WE ALL DIE IN THE END

(Scenes from a Small Town)

ELIZABETH MERRY

For My Family

We All Die in the End ·

(Scenes from a Small Town)

Copyright © 2020 Elizabeth Merry

ISBN-9798689101705

Cover design by designforwriters.com

Many thanks to Clare Murray and Siobhán Devoy for their invaluable help in formatting and proof-reading this book.

The following stories have previously been published in Literary Magazines and newspapers, or have been broadcast on National Radio:

Jemima; Andy; Arthur Swann; Siblings; Wee Sadie; Rosemary; Dolly; Paulie; Julia; Myrtle; Pet; May Toal; Thelma; Man and Wife; Eugene Curran.

Quotes from reviews:

"Elizabeth Merry's characters leap from the page, fully formed. Within a few paragraphs, I can visualize them in my mind . . . the book is well edited, and the prose is perfect." *Jean M Roberts, Author, Genealogist, Historian.*

"Merry's is some of the best writing I've read in a while. We All Die in the End has left me with a haunting literary hangover. And for that, I am grateful. For, as rare as it is, it is that exact after effect I yearn for in every book I read." *Kurt Brindley, Author, Reviewer.*

"The writing is polished, and the characters are deeply rendered and distinct . . . Each story is unique. Highly recommended to short story readers and readers of literary fiction." *D Wallace Peach, Novelist, Blogger, Reviewer.*

www.embookstuff.wordpress.com

Twitter @elizabethmerry1

Arthur Swann

The first day I saw Lydia I knew that here was a woman I could help. Of course I didn't know then her name was Lydia. She was just a small, fair-haired woman carrying a doll - one of those great big baby dolls. I was quite annoyed when I saw her actually. There's never anybody on that part of the beach; there's no sand, you know, it's all shingle, and I like to have my head to myself. I was just standing there having a smoke and watching the waves when she appeared. Freezing, it was that day; when I blew out smoke, I didn't know how much was smoke and how much my breath in the cold air.

I usually walk there for an hour or two - that's what I do in the afternoons. My days are carefully measured out - one of them head doctors recommended that and it works fine for me. So many hours for resting, so many for exercise, and then there's mealtimes and going to the shops, and there you are, another day got through safely.

Although, mind you, I often stay out just to escape Jennifer - that's my neighbour. She has these dogs, and she's all over you - you have to lean back when she's talking to you. She takes an interest in me - that's how she puts it - I'd put it another way myself; I think she has her eye on me for a fancy man, living with dogs as she does and no man to herself. Ha! And I have another neighbour wears yellow all the time, a young one, she is, nothing but yellow, and drives a wee, yellow car. But there you are, sure there's mad people everywhere.

However, as I was saying, it's the routine; I need the routine, it keeps me from gathering up the pills and buying that final bottle of booze. I know, I know, mustn't mention that word - mustn't even let it form in my mind. It's gone, there - I've forgotten it.

I avoid going past my old local of course, Dinnie's that was, Julia's now I suppose. That's the daughter, but everyone still calls it Dinnie's. Ah, the warmth of that oul pub, the smell, the craic, myself and Eugene Curran and the Grimley brothers, my old boozing buddies - I try to avoid them too but that's not easy here in this wee town - half a dozen streets and the very long and very twisty Hunter's Lane where I live myself and that's the whole of it - sure you see everybody. And what was so terrible about that old life after all? Now, now, now, that'll do.

So, I watched Lydia and waited for some bloody nuisance of a child to come screeching after her but no child came. Well, that didn't make any sense but then Lydia stopped and I saw her speak to the doll. Oho, Arthur, I said to myself and I threw down the cigarette. Oho, I said, what's this? What have we here?

I walked nearer to her but I couldn't hear what she was saying without going too close. I saw her point at the sea and brush her cheek across the hard brown curls on the doll's head. Ah, you poor, mad cratur, I thought and I went up behind her. I was much taller and thinner than she was and I leaned over her protectively but she turned and jumped away, throwing me a look as she went.

2

What did she want to look at me like that for? Like I was going to bite her or something. It pisses me off when people are suspicious like that. I stood my ground and then I turned and stared after her. Why shouldn't I stare at her? Hadn't I every right to stand there and put my face where I liked? I thought about her eyes, small and sad. I was going to follow her that first day but I was tired somehow so I sat on my usual rock and lit another smoke.

The last few months have been tough, you know. It's not always easy. You needn't think it's easy to motivate myself. I do the mental exercises - say the right words - but it's like I'm not listening sometimes, and then I just lie around all day. I listen to the radio and I keep the curtains closed. Jennifer knocks but I don't answer. The thing is - it always passes and I get up again.

And I remember what I've been told, that I should try to help others and not be feeling sorry for myself. It's easy for others to talk, people with families, cars, holidays, all that. What do they know about routine and exercises and watching every word that comes into your own head? Oh, Arthur, I say to myself. Where did you go wrong? Well, I know the answer to that one all right.

Anyway . . . It was two weeks before I saw Lydia again (having gone through a bit of a bad patch) and I said to myself, oho, Arthur, there she is, poor soul, a woman who lost a baby if ever I saw one. It was obvious, wasn't it? She was holding the doll again, tight under her arm. You see, other people wouldn't notice a thing like that - they would just assume there was a child with her. But I'm different – I pay attention. I kept my distance this time, happy to be back by the sea. It was a cold, calm day and the sea was blue and quiet. I sat on my rock and stared out at a ship moving slowly against the horizon and when Lydia turned to go back up the street, I followed her. It would help me to help her and that was a fair exchange.

Well, it was the strangest thing and it made no sense at all but I thought she was going to my house. She wasn't, of course; she went straight on up Main Street to one of the wee terrace houses. To think I'd never seen her before and her living right here under my nose! Of course I've been away for a long while but all the same, I'd have thought I knew all the faces.

When she went into her house I sauntered past and back a few times and then I went to sit on the low wall opposite and have a smoke. I studied the house; the paint was a bit tired looking but the curtains were white. Poor woman, I thought, with a little dead baby. Maybe she had a collection of pills too and a bottle of that which cannot be mentioned.

I ground out the fag and stood up and right then the curtain moved in the front room. I was sure of it and I stood still for a minute. I lifted my hand to my eyes and peered up and down like I was waiting for someone, and then I thought - so what if she had seen me anyway? I wasn't hiding, was I? I was entitled to sit on the public wall if I liked - in fact, she had no business nosing around the curtain like that.

I imagined the small, sad eyes watching me. She would be standing to one side and the doll would be lying in a cot beside her or in a pram and she'd be rocking it. Poor Lydia - still, she'd no call to be staring out like that. I looked directly at the window and strolled across the street

4

to the gate. It was a small gate, painted blue, and I put my hand on it. I gave it a bit of a push, just to show her, and then I went home. Well, I knew what I'd have to do. I'd have to ask Jennifer, dogs or not. If there was anything going on that Jennifer didn't know about, then it wasn't going on at all. Now, Arthur, I said to myself - be brave.

The dogs hurled themselves out the door and over my feet, yelping and yipping and I had to force myself to stand still. Jennifer beamed at me.

"Arthur!"

She leaned forward and her hand snaked out to pull me in.

"Where have you been?" she cried.

"Can't stop, Jennifer," I said, leaning back. "Just called to say hello."

There was no way I was going inside that house. People have been known to go in there and never come out again. Well, I'm exaggerating but you know what I mean. I asked her how she was and I let her talk away to herself and when I couldn't stick it any longer, I said to her:

"Now, Jennifer, you're a wise woman who sees all and knows all."

I knew she'd like that and indeed she smirked at me, and then I asked her did she ever see a woman about the place carrying a doll.

"Ah," she said. "Oh, indeed. That's poor Lydia, she's not all there."

Her fingers nipped and dug into my arm.

"Very sad case, terrible altogether. Of course the husband had every right, you know. Sure you couldn't leave a child with the likes of that."

"The likes of what?" I said.

"Well, it wasn't her fault - she couldn't help it. The poor woman didn't know what she was doing - out in the middle of the night in her night-dress - just standing there in the garden - hadn't a clue where she was and the child bawling inside the house. One day, she left the pram outside the paper-shop. She was always crying too, cried a lot, so she did."

I was beginning to wonder if Lydia had the same affliction as myself when Jennifer pulled me closer. I stepped back, my foot feeling for the edge of the step.

"Nerves," Jennifer said. "The husband has a job abroad, Brussels, something to do with taxes, took the child off. He has one of them au pairs to mind her."

I had to practically tear Jennifer's hand off my arm and promise to have tea the next time and all that and, by God, I needed a smoke to restore myself. I was a bit disappointed the baby wasn't dead, being usually right as I am. A girl to mind the baby indeed. It makes no sense at all but I imagined her as Dutch, long yellow plaits and a big skirt. I'm a little Dutch girl, she'd sing to the baby and when it was asleep, Lydia's husband would go up and stand behind her and undo the plaits.

I couldn't sleep that night. I smoked so many fags I couldn't take another drag, just light up and hold the thing and flick the ashes. I got dressed early and ate my bit of toast and I drank my orange juice. You see? I do what I'm told. I get my vitamins. I listened to the radio for a bit; not music though, the news, I like the news. Can't stand that caterwauling early in the morning.

I still hadn't any plan how to help Lydia but I felt I should be near her house in case I thought of something. The sky was overcast and there wasn't much of a wind but now and again a breeze found me out and I pulled my scarf tighter. I feel the cold something awful. Of course I was well wrapped up, but even so.

The street was quiet when I went round; everybody gone to work obviously - no cars about. Lydia's curtains were open. I couldn't tell if she was in or out and I wondered if I could get down the side and round the back of the house. She might be in the kitchen at this hour. She'd be eating cornflakes and there'd be a bowl of something in front of the doll, propped in a baby's high chair. I could see the side door was rotten, the wood breaking apart - one good kick would do it. I opened the gate - it didn't make a sound - and I went and listened at the front door. Now, Arthur, I said to myself. What are you going to do? If she's in, I thought, I'll say I'm from the residents; start from there . . . right. I flicked my fag away and knocked the door. Nothing. I knocked again and stood back and looked at the windows and just when I was beginning to think about how to break in, the door opened.

"Yes?" she said.

She had a very loud, deep voice for such a small person and I stared at her for a minute, not sure how to begin. And then I saw a look coming into her eyes and I knew she recognised me from sitting across the road the day before. I was just about to say my name when she closed over the door.

"Go away!" she said through the inch left open. "What do you want? Get away from here! I'll call the police!"

Well, that was enough. The bloody cheek of her. And asking me what did I want and telling me to get away at the same time. But sure the woman wasn't right. I forced the door open and stood on the threshold and she pushed me back and started crying, and only for I heard voices on the road, I'd have shaken a bit of sense into her right there on the spot. But I had to jump back down the step and of course she slammed the door.

I went to the park then and did a bit of running myself . . . well, I didn't actually run, more of a fast walk. Did you ever notice about exercise? You hate the thought of it and then you end up liking it. Round and round the park I went, worrying about Lydia. There was only one thing for it - she'd have to lose that doll. Cold turkey! It's terrible at first but it works; it works; amn't I the man knows that only too well?

So, after lunch - bread and fruit and a lump of cheese - I went down to the sea. If Lydia was a creature of habit like the rest of us she'd be there around the same time so I lit a fag and sat on my rock. I kept my gloves on for the cold was biting. Did you ever try to smoke with gloves on? It isn't easy but you get used to it. As my old Da used to say - you can get used to anything, even hanging.

I saw Lydia from far off and I took a deep drag on my cigarette and moved back where she couldn't see me;

no use scaring her off before I got a chance to get the doll. I was breathing fast and my hands were hot now inside the gloves.

Here she came, clutching the doll, its head with the plastic curl tucked under her chin. Poor, sorry cratur. Well, her troubles would soon be over. She looked around her a bit - jumpy, she was. There were a couple of kids further up which annoyed me; we'd need a bit of privacy for our chat. I would speak softly to her and tell her my name - people who want to threaten don't tell you their names, do they? So, I'd make her feel easy and she'd know I wanted to help her.

She stopped and looked out to sea like she had before and I stamped out the butt of my fag and went straight over to her

"Hello," I said softly, bending down and speaking into her ear. "It's me - "

Before I could say anything else she squealed and jumped like she was scalded.

"Go away!" she said. "What do you want? Go away!"

Her face was squeezed like she was going to cry and I thought to myself, Oho, Arthur, you'll have to work quickly here if you're going to help this poor woman. I grabbed the doll from under her arm and ran to the litter bin up near the road, and what did she do only come after me, shrieking like a banshee, the two of us slipping and tripping on the shingle.

"Shut up!" I said, close to her face, and I have to say I was really pissed off with the noise she was making. People would hear her; there'd be a fuss. The head wouldn't go through the slot and I pressed it down until I felt it crack and I shoved it harder. Lydia was clawing at me and crying.

"Shut up, you stupid, looney bitch!"

There's only so much you can take after all and I'm in a delicate condition and not allowed to mention certain things and I don't need to be upset. People were gathering around like flies. Where had they come from? The doll fell through into the bin and Lydia crumpled up in a heap on the ground. Such hysterics! I could see I'd be no help to her right at that minute and I was pushed aside as more people stopped to look, asking each other, what happened, and saying, that's poor Lydia, poor Lydia, that's all I could hear, poor Lydia.

Well, she'd get better now anyway without the doll. One of these days she'd be knocking on my door to say thanks.

I thought I'd go home for a while and have a rest and then I heard someone say she'd been assaulted. Assaulted! Did you ever hear the like? Is there any sense left in this world at all? And that's slander, so it is - I never laid a finger on her. And sure what about it if I had? What does it matter? What does any of it matter? We all die in the end.

Carmel

I remember being really happy that Sunday when I first mentioned the picnic. The Summer had properly begun and I was wearing the powder blue. We were walking near the lighthouse eating ice-cream and everybody was lifted by the sunshine and the heat.

With any luck I'd be able to stop taking the cough medicine soon, although my Summer allergies were nearly as bad. But I was looking well, I must say - the little bit of weight helped me - and I had a fine looking man on either side of me. One was my brother and the other our dear, old friend, Billy Woods; Billy was a retired solicitor and I had been his secretary for many years. Indeed there was a time, long ago, when I thought that Billy and I might . . . but there you are, it never happened.

We were strolling along, just chatting, Billy telling one of his yarns, and I thought wouldn't it be nice if the three of us could go on a picnic, somewhere up the coast road maybe, so I said it to the men, looking up into their broad, healthy faces.

"Great idea," Billy said.

"Not today though, I've a meeting later on."

"No, of course," I said. "Some weekend that suits us all."

"I'm ready for anything," Aidan said.

11

He tapped at his chin as he spoke - he was always doing that. Dark stubble pricked his face an hour after shaving. I told him once it reminded me of the yard brushes at the back of our shop. He even smelled of them, of the brushes and the nails and the mats. Well the shop was home and its smell was home too so that was all right.

I was so happy thinking about the picnic and I didn't realise Jennifer was anywhere near until her two dogs starting nosing around us. One of them licked my fingers and I wiped them on a tissue.

"There you are, Carmel," she said, grabbing hold of my arm. "Did I hear you say a picnic? Oh, wouldn't I love that! I do love a trip. Would you be going soon? Oh, I'd love to go."

"Well, I'm off or I'll be late," Billy said. "But remind me, Carmel, during the week, send me a text."

And then he was gone and the dogs were snuffling and yapping. Aidan was patting at them and saying, good boy, good boy.

Jennifer stood there smiling at me, waiting for me to go on about the picnic. She was wearing a sleeveless pink blouse and a short skirt and her arms and legs were nearly green they were that pale. Her hair was the colour of redbrick that week - it was always some peculiar shade of red. I don't know why she liked me - she was always hanging around, her and her dogs. She smelled of them and there were long hairs on her clothes. Every time we met her she invited me to tea in her house but I never went - the allergies would kill me, and how could you eat anything?

"Jennifer," I said. "I didn't see you there. We were just talking . . . "

"Yes."

Jennifer moved closer, grabbing and squeezing at my arm.

"A picnic - you said a picnic - up the coast."

Aidan was oblivious, playing with the dogs, trying to make them sit and lie down and all that. I backed away from her, conscious of my fresh powder blue.

"No, no," I said. "That was only a thought - it wasn't . . . I mean - there wasn't anything definite."

Jennifer looked at the ground. I could feel the warm sun on my back and I moved my shoulders and wished she would go away. She didn't say anything for a minute and then she turned and called the dogs and I relaxed. She went quickly out to the street with the dogs behind her and Aidan rubbed his bristles.

"She's a wonder, that wee woman, isn't she? All on her own like that. She knits you know, earns a bit of money for herself. She's a - "

"Yes, Aidan, yes, yes, I know. Don't keep going on about her."

When it was tea-time I brought out the goodies and set them on the table making everything nice for Aidan. He was reading the paper in the garden, his head nodding under the white hat. I had lemon tarts and chocolate fingers and I didn't feel a bit guilty about taking them. After all, I had to be careful with my pension and Aidan didn't make a fortune in the shop. He gave me as much for housekeeping as he could and he was so fond of something sweet.

I reasoned it out like this - if a man is starving and he steals a loaf, is there anything wrong with that? Not at all. So, if Aidan works hard in the shop and I work very hard in the house - is it wrong of me to add something to my shopping basket? Besides everybody knows that Higgins is a crook and would charge you extra if he could and often did, so I took tarts and biscuits and other goodies with an easy mind. There'd be more choice in the supermarket of course but I never went there - too many cameras. I called Aidan in to tea then and never gave Jennifer another thought.

*

It was two weeks later and the weather had held. The sun burned fiercely and Aidan wore his white hat all the time. The smell in the shop grew stronger every day - it was the yard-brushes with their hard orange bristles. I'm sure those bristles were dipped in something poisonous. I kept all the windows open and used plenty of rose air-freshener, and I kept my tissues fresh with lavender oil. It was terrifically hot so I decided on a cold meat salad for the tea and off I went to the butcher`s.

I wore tan sandals and a yellow sun-dress and my arms were plump and covered with freckles. Such a pity the young ones don't wear nice clothes - parading around in those skin-tight leggings with every inch of their wee bottoms on show, some not so wee either. There was a great smell of grass and nettles from the ditch at the corner - I breathed it in and I was happy thinking about teatime. Only the butcher's shop is a trial on a hot day. Now the butcher is a very nice man, George MacBride, he just got married to wee Sadie Hughes, her mother is an old friend of mine, and the shop is very clean, but, oh, the smell of meat! It would almost put you off your steak. I thought then about ice-cream, banana ice-cream, so cold, so sweet, and I turned down the street to Higgins`.

There were a few people standing about in the shop, poking at the magazines and that. I bought a packet of tissues and said good-afternoon to them all. The fridge was over to the side and I waited until I heard Higgins talking and the till rattling and then I reached in and lifted the banana ice-cream. He had a camera too of course but only one and it was pointed at the door.

I dropped the ice-cream into my basket and turned to go and there was Jennifer! Just standing there looking at me! I was frozen - I couldn't move and I couldn't speak. Her hair was pink and she wore a dress with red flowers on it. I moved my lips but no words came out.

"There you are, Carmel," she said slowly.

"Lovely day," she said and stared at the basket.

"Are you doing a bit of shopping?"

"Yes." I got the word out.

And then I came unstuck and started moving and talking all at once.

"Gorgeous day. Aren't we lucky now with the weather? And how are you keeping yourself, Jennifer? We hardly see you these days. Doesn't everybody look better in the Summer? I always think that. Wouldn't it be lovely to live in a hot place? I mean a nice, warm place like Spain or Italy, or Greece maybe. Don't you think that would be nice?"

And all the time I was talking, I was walking, faster and faster until I was nearly running. The dogs were padding around me and Jennifer bobbed away at my shoulder. I couldn't get rid of her. We stopped outside our shop and I was panting.

"Must go in now," I said. "Work to do, work to do."

I could see Aidan leaning over the counter to see who I was with but I went in the house door and shut it and sank to the floor. I don't know how long I sat there but I got up at last, thinking about the banana ice-cream melting in the basket. I went up the stairs and put it in the fridge and about half an hour later Aidan came up and said we'd be having a visitor for tea.

"What?" I said. "Is it Billy?"

He did come in sometimes for his tea and if it was him I'd have to go back out again and get some chocolate biscuits or something and to tell the truth I didn't feel I'd be able. The table was set for two but I could change that easy enough and there were plenty of sandwiches made.

"No, no," Aidan said. "It's that wee woman, Jennifer."

I just stared at him. The bristles on his chin were bright in the sun and suddenly I felt too hot. I sat down and Aidan asked me what was wrong.

"I don't know," I said.

"You won't mind that wee woman having tea with us, will you? Sure we always have plenty, don't we dear? She came in to the shop - weren't you talking to her yourself outside there? She came in when you went upstairs. She didn't buy anything but she walked around having a look. She said she might be putting up a shelf or two and one thing led to another. She's a lonely, wee cratur I think – so, well I suppose I invited her. She'll be here soon."

And didn't the doorbell ring at that minute and I squealed and Aidan asked me again was I all right.

"It's the heat maybe, Carmel," he said and he fanned me with a magazine. "I'll let her up," he said. "You don't move."

But I got up and put another setting on the white tablecloth and then in came Jennifer, all smiles with her pink hair and the dress with red flowers.

"There you are, Carmel," she said and I shivered.

She looked all around the room, taking everything in.

"Oh, look at your telly," she said. "It's huge!"

"My only luxury," Aidan said, "for the sport, you know."

"The sport . . . even tennis?"

Jennifer stared at the television.

"Certainly the tennis," Aidan said.

"I love the tennis," Jennifer said. "But it's hard to see it properly on a small telly. I only have a small one."

"Well, you can watch it here, can't she, Carmel? No problem at all, you'd be welcome."

Aidan sat down and waved her to a seat and I went into the kitchen to wet the tea. I knew my face was white. You can always tell - you can feel the blood leaving your head. I couldn't think what to do. I liked the tennis myself, and to think of her sitting on our couch . . . no, I wouldn't be able to bear it."

"Tea!" Aidan shouted from the table. "We're dying of thirst in here."

He didn't mind Jennifer a bit. He liked company - anybody at all. He'd talk to people in the shop for hours and then they'd only buy a screwdriver or something. I brought in the teapot and started talking very quickly like I had before. It seemed to be the only way I could get through the minutes. Maybe I thought that if I kept talking she wouldn't get a chance to say anything so I went on and on about nothing. Aidan had stopped talking. He was a hungry man and ate a lot of food, and normally I'd be the same.

"I know!" Jennifer jumped in when I took a breath. "You must come to my house - some day next week. I'll bake scones, and I could knit you a jumper, Carmel. I like knitting, so I do, I do it all the time."

"Well, it's very kind of you - isn't it very kind of her, Carmel?"

Aidan waved his knife across the table.

"I couldn't go of course - I have the shop, but Carmel can go."

I felt sick. I was shaking and I put down my cup. It rattled and I held it tight with both hands. All I could think of was the inside of Jennifer's house. It would be dark - the windows would be shut and the dogs would put their heads on my knee. There'd be dog-hairs all over my clothes and the smell would make me ill. I thought of a jumper knitted with dog-hairs instead of wool and I could feel the beginnings of a horrible, hysterical laugh.

Jennifer was staring at me, waiting for me to say when I would come but I couldn't speak. I was swallowing the giggle and I wondered if I was going to faint because the table was blurred and Aidan seemed to be making an awful lot of noise with the knife, and then Jennifer mentioned the picnic.

"Yes," Aidan wiped his mouth. "You did say something about a picnic, Carmel. Do you remember? Ourselves and Billy . . . "

He stopped and looked at Jennifer.

"And yourself too - you'd be welcome, wouldn't she, Carmel? Plenty of room in the car. And sure isn't the weather perfect for it? We'll do it - we'll go on Sunday if Billy's free and Carmel will look after the goodies - no better woman and I say it myself even if she is my own sister."

Jennifer smiled and lifted her chin at me. She said she loved a trip, and then she said a bit of ice-cream would be nice. The sweat broke on me and I jumped up from the table.

"Ice-cream!" I shouted, and Aidan looked at me. "Of course! How could I forget the ice-cream?"

I laughed out loud and went into the kitchen and spooned the banana ice-cream into three dishes.

"Lovely," Jennifer said, lingering over each spoonful.

"Just lovely. Perfect."

*

I wanted to say I was sick on Sunday morning but I hadn't the nerve. We had to pick up Billy and Jennifer at mid-day. I wrapped sandwiches in tinfoil, and chicken in cling-film. Then Aidan said you couldn't have a picnic without strawberries so I got them. It was easy enough - there were a lot of people in buying newspapers. Aidan put a bottle of white wine in the boot in the cool bag and a couple of beers for himself and then we were ready.

Billy was in great form and his big, broad face was shiny. He was wearing a suit, even in the heat; he always said he'd got used to wearing it over the years and couldn't leave it off. He sat in the front beside Aidan, he said he got sick if he sat in the back, and then he began to tell Aidan a yarn about something but I didn't listen. We drove down Hunter's Lane and Jennifer came out of her dingy-looking house - she had pink lace curtains at the single window - pink curtains! We could hear her shouting instructions to the dogs inside. She got in beside me and I wound the window down as far as it would go.

Billy rumbled on in the front and I stared out the window. God knows it was nice enough out there to keep anybody looking. The sea below was so blue, pale and navy-blue and green as well.

Jennifer was wearing a peculiar cream-coloured, floaty sort of dress and there were definitely dog-hairs on it. I sat tight against the side of the car with my face to the breeze. The panic had worn off me a bit and I felt more angry than scared.

Maybe, I tried to fool myself, maybe she hadn't noticed that day, or maybe she thought I had already paid for the ice-cream. I closed my eyes and Billy went on and on and Aidan said yes and yes and wasn't that a wonder.

"Isn't a car a blessing?" Jennifer said. "I never learned to drive myself."

Her face was as pink as her hair and she leaned over towards me. I was afraid I might have to push her back or something and then Aidan stopped the car.

"Will this do?" he asked, turning around to us. "Carmel - is this the spot marked x?"

"Yes," I said, realising where we were.

There were other cars parked nearby, families with children - I hoped they wouldn't be noisy. I wanted to stay in the car and hide myself but I had to get out and smile and see to the food. Billy wiped his face and took off his jacket and Aidan wiped his head and asked me where was his hat. I spread the rug on the sandy grass and unpacked the picnic.

Jennifer's eyes darted over everything and she sat down in the floaty dress. The sun burned on her pink scalp through her pink hair and I hoped she'd get sunstroke. She looked at the strawberries and smiled.

"Strawberries," she said. "Gorgeous - so expensive though."

Aidan ate a couple of them.

"Are they so?" he asked. "Well, that's no matter. Our Carmel is a wonder - she's an absolute wonder. She manages the house like silk. They should have her in the government - she'd organise their budget for them. There'd be no talk of the national debt then. We'd all have strawberries if Carmel was in charge. Strawberries for all - every day!"

Oh, Aidan was enjoying himself. Billy sank onto the tartan rug and spread a white napkin on his knee. He heaped it with chicken and sandwiches and began another story and Aidan said yes and yes and is that the truth, he was good at doing that.

We opened the wine and drank it from plastic cups. It didn't taste great but I really needed it and poured plenty into my own cup.

I stretched my plump, freckled arms out in front of me and thought what a shame it was - the lovely day and the food and the cool breeze all wasted because of Jennifer. I jumped when she spoke again.

"The next time," she said to me, "we could go to The Giant's Causeway - I've never been there. That would be good, wouldn't it, Carmel?"

She waited for my reply. The blood ran about in my head and I couldn't swallow. I chewed slowly and tried to think of something to say.

"Oh, I don't know," I said. "Aidan can't always get away, the shop - "

"It's closed on Sundays," she said, quick as anything.

"Yes, but . . . " I floundered, "there's st-st-stocktaking. That has to be done on Sundays, and then," I speeded up now, "he has to tidy the shelves - all those nails."

Jennifer set down her chicken and turned to the men.

"Billy," she said. "Are there any laws about working on Sundays, you know how many hours you can work and all that?"

"And that was the last time I ever - sorry? What was that, Jennifer?"

Billy turned himself around and he raised his eyebrows at Jennifer.

"I was asking about the laws on working hours, Billy," Jennifer said. "Carmel was telling me that poor Aidan has to tidy up the shop on Sundays and we mightn't be able to have any more rides in the motor."

Aidan looked at me but I kept my head down. I twisted and twisted my napkin until it was a string in my lap. Billy laughed.

"Ah, no," he said, rubbing his chin although he didn't have midday bristles like Aidan.

"Sure it's Aidan's own business and if he has to do things on a Sunday that - "

"But I don't - " Aidan began.

"No law against that whatsoever."

"And what about theft, Billy?"

I screamed and made to get up and Aidan reached out a hand to me.

"It's all right," I said. "There was a wasp in the strawberries."

There were in fact a lot of wasps about and I was going to say we should go home but I thought that if we stayed Jennifer might get stung on the tongue and choke to death, or maybe she would really get sunstroke. I waved my hand over the food and fussed around but Jennifer didn't stop.

"Well, Billy?" she said.

Billy brushed crumbs off his shirt front.

"What are you asking me, Jennifer?" he said, frowning.

"About theft," Jennifer said, sitting up very straight. "Would you go to jail for - say - stealing ice-cream?"

My heart began a slow thumping that I could hear. I was hot and cold together and it was like when she caught me first - I was frozen.

"Unlikely," Billy said. "Very unlikely. There's worse things in the world than you can imagine, Jennifer."

"Well, if you knew someone was stealing are you obliged to report it?"

Billy gave a bit of a laugh.

"You're beginning to interest me, Jennifer. What have you been up to?"

Jennifer opened her mouth to speak again but I couldn't bear it. I leapt to my feet and almost did a dance on the spot. Billy and Aidan both got up and Aidan fanned me with his white hat.

"Carmel . . . what . . . Carmel, dear, sit down, sit down."

"Too hot," Billy said.

"Her allergies," Aidan said.

My knees were trembling and I knew there were tears on my face. I half-fell to the tartan rug.

"I'm all right, thanks. I don't know what came over me. I'm fine now, really. Don't worry Aidan."

I looked at Jennifer.

"Yes, I'm sure we could manage another trip before the Summer's over. We could go . . . "

But I couldn't say another word. My limbs felt heavy and my head drooped and Jennifer's fingers closed around my wrist.

"We'll go in the car again," she said. "And I`ll knit you a jumper - blue, I think, blue and cream. Do you want that last sandwich?"

I shook my head and lay back and the sun was very hot on my face and arms. There is always such comfort in heat.

Wee Sadie

Even with the heating on Madge liked the fire lit. It burned fiercely at Sadie's feet and she dozed and dreamed with her book open on her knee. She imagined the heat of the desert and the hot, spicy smell. It would be like cinnamon, she thought, or cloves. And if she was there, she would be beautiful; the heat would smooth out the kinks in her hair and a handsome, foreign man would take her to dinner and give her wine, and later he would lead her up the curving staircase to the bedroom . . .

She was aware of noises from the kitchen, the television and the clink of glass and bottle; her mother was on her second gin and would be looking for her dinner soon.

When she rose her new skirt with the tiny pleats swung out and she twirled on the red carpet and pointed her toes and looked towards the mirror. Looking good, our Sadie, she said to herself. I'd nearly pass for sixteen still. She laughed aloud and fluffed out her hair – the blonde highlights were good. There was silence from the kitchen now and she fell back onto the couch, reaching for her book again.

"Sadie!"

She got up and went into the kitchen. There was a cut lemon beside the gin bottle and the smell was sharp.

"I know, Mammy. I know."

She lit the gas and swung the frying-pan across the flames.

"Good girl." Madge swallowed gin. "Good girl."

Sadie said nothing. She trimmed the fat of the kidneys and the liver, her fingers curling away from the soft, red slither and she held her breath against the faint smell of blood. Madge lifted her walking-stick and rattled it against the leg of the table.

"What's the matter with you, miss?

"What's the matter with you, miss? What have you a face on you for? Turning your nose up at a decent bit of meat. If you're after fillet steak you know what to do!"

Sadie half turned from the cooker and eyed her mother. Was she going to start on about George again? She separated sausages and threw the lot on the pan and then her phoned beeped on the worktop; that would be Hannah about meeting up later.

"That yoke squawking again! That flighty article, Hannah, I suppose, off to the pub again. You're a scatterbrain," Madge said. "Reading them silly novels, staring in the mirror, waiting for what, I'd like to know. If you'd even look for a better job - stuck in that supermarket - or learn to drive and your father's car sitting out there like an ornament. If he was still alive . . . "

Madge touched her eyes with a tissue and Sadie jabbed at the kidneys.

"Such good times we had in that car, going for a drive on Sundays, and you sitting so quiet in the back with your hair in blue ribbons."

A tear slid onto Madge's hand.

"And now look at you! Nearly thirty and nothing to show for it!"

"Mammy! I'm twenty-six!"

"That was old when I was a girl! You should marry the butcher, that George MacBride. I've seen him looking at you in the shop. Do you think I don't notice? Holding onto your hand giving you the change, bits of honest blood stuck to his fingers."

Madge thumped her stick on the floor.

"Well, what about it? Can`t you encourage him a bit!"

Sadie turned the liver on the pan and shook her head.

"No!" she said. "No! The cheek of him to look at me!"

"Your head's full of nonsense out of them books. That butcher's a fine, young man - I never heard a bad word about him. He's shy and he doesn't say much but that's no harm - and think of the meat, Sadie. Steak and roast and chops, nice bit of stuffed pork on a Sunday . . . "

Sadie banged a drawer. She set the table and thought about the butcher. He'd started coming to the pub on Saturday nights but she wasn't going to tell her mother that. He always sat near herself and Hannah and he always bought them a drink but he never talked, only beamed when she looked straight at him. He smelled of baby-powder and his hair was slick with gel and she was pleased with the attention, but still . . .

"Throw some bread on the pan there," Madge said, and poured herself another gin.

*

Hannah pulled at Sadie's arm.

"Look who's coming in the door this very minute!"

It was Saturday night and they were on their first glass of wine. Sadie wasn't looking but she knew exactly where George was standing and she was annoyed with herself for knowing.

"I will not look! I'm not going to take him under my notice. You're as bad as Mammy."

"Julia says he's dying about you, she says he never takes his eyes off you. He's terrible shy though. There's men like that, it's a problem sometimes."

Sadie shook her head. She almost wished he fancied Hannah instead but he never looked at Hannah, and she had a man anyway, even if he was married. And that smell of baby powder! Sadie often felt that if she tapped George's chest a cloud of it would fly out and choke her.

And then he was there, right beside them, pulling over a stool. Well this was a new departure as her old teacher used to say. She looked closer at him; his eyes were very blue and she wondered what colour his hair would be without the gel.

30

"What about you, George?"

The words surprised her; she hadn't meant to speak to him.

"I'm grand, sure, just grand," George said.

Sadie was aware of Hannah trying not to laugh beside her. She jumped when George touched her hand.

"Sadie," he said. "Sadie . . . could we talk? Would you come outside - for a minute? Is that all right, Hannah? Julia's bringing you over a drink."

"Of course, George, thanks," Hannah said.

Sadie could feel Hannah`s elbow digging into her. She had never heard George say a whole sentence before and she didn't know what to say herself but she lifted her bag and jacket and followed him outside.

"Let`s go for a bit of a walk," he said. "I can`t hear myself thinking in there, all the shouting, your man Curran and the brothers . . . "

"Aye, the brothers Grimm," Sadie said with a nervous laugh.

George took her hand and looked at her to see if it was all right. She didn't pull away and they walked slowly down the main street as far as the sea wall before they turned back. Sadie kept her head down, wondering if George was ever going to say another word. She was sure that the whole town was looking at them, but it was a good feeling at the same time and her fingers moved in George's warm hand.

"Sadie," he said at last. "I've been meaning to, to ask . . . I'm sure you know I like you, very much, and I thought we might - I might - take you out - if you would like."

Sadie couldn't answer. She nodded and he held her hand tighter and after a while he walked her back up the street to Dinnie's.

"Can I phone you tomorrow?" he asked. "I've got a new one," he said, taking it out of his pocket.

"Rosemary set it up for me. She's my aunt but we get on the very best, you'd maybe see her about the beach, she wears white all the time, you'd notice her. And she does the books for me at the shop, calls herself my tech support."

George laughed and Sadie laughed too; his eyes were really very blue.

"I don't be down there that often," Sadie said then. "All the stones you know, it's not a good beach."

"Not for those wee shoes," George said, pressing her arm to his side.

"Will you give me your number so? We could go for something to eat if you like, and a couple of drinks?"

"Oh . . . all right," Sadie said.

She saw him nearly every day after that and they got used to each other. George still didn't say much but he seemed to be easy in her company and she got very fond of him. They walked along the sea, and sometimes he met her for lunch if the shop wasn't too busy, and at night they went to the pictures or the pub. She told Hannah she'd never seen so many movies in her life; George was mad for them, she said.

*

"Mammy, will you not drink tonight? Just this evening, until George goes home. And leave the telly off."

"Ashamed of your mother, is that it?"

Madge rapped the cooker with her stick.

"Well, it comes to us all, I suppose. If your poor father - "

"Mammy! Stop it! You know I don't mean that at all. It's just that . . . he's not going to be here long, only for his tea."

Sadie opened the shopping bag.

"I got Greek salad - and I got a coffee cake –he likes coffee cake."

"Money for rubbish! What else did you get? Are you going to feed a butcher with salad? He won't eat that. You'll soon learn when you're married he'll be - "

"Mammy! He hasn't asked - he hasn't said anything."

"He's old-fashioned - he'll probably ask me first. Don't rush to bring the tea in when he gets here - give the man a chance to say what he has to say."

"Don't you - Mammy - you wouldn't - "

"Don't be daft."

Madge watched lettuce and cheese and olives appear on the table.

"Do I have to eat that too?" she said.

"Well, of course you do, the three of us. He's coming for tea - he eats his dinner early, so . . . and I got good bread too."

Madge sighed.

"The things I do for you, my girl. I'm going to have one gin - "

"Ah, Mammy."

"It doesn't smell. If I have to eat that stuff I need one, or two. He won't see it. I won't drink it at the table. And you can do me a decent fry later."

Sadie washed the lettuce and tossed the salad and sliced the bread and Madge downed a large gin. The doorbell made them both jump.

"He's here, am I all right? Do I look all right?"

"You look fine. Doesn't he know what you look like? Leave off at that mirror. Are you going to leave him standing out there?"

Madge rose and went into the sitting-room, leaning heavily on the stick and then George came into the room behind Sadie, beaming and ducking his head.

"There you are now, George," Madge said. "You're welcome in this house. Sit down now, sit yourself down."

"Thanks, Mrs Hughes."

George sat into the softness of the couch and Sadie hovered, her hands darting around the cushions until Madge said the tea would be ready in a minute and shooed her off to the kitchen.

"Would you like a drink first, George? There's gin or - "

"Ah no, no thanks, Mrs Hughes. Tea is fine."

Sadie checked the plates, shifting bits of cheese and cherry tomatoes. She ate a crust of the bread and put the kettle on and then she stood with her ear to the door.

"It's a grand, wee flat above the shop," George was saying.

Sadie squeezed her eyes shut and held her breath. Madge was asking how many rooms there were. The kettle hissed behind her and she turned down the gas to hear better.

"And I'd expect a bit of meat, you know, and maybe a drive on a Sunday. You can have that oul car, parked out there, teach Sadie to drive it."

Sadie raised the gas again. Her hands trembled as she filled the teapot. Calm, she told herself, be calm. But the tray shook when she took in the tea and she couldn't look at either one of them. The knives and forks clattered and the teaspoons rattled and Sadie couldn't swallow.

"Have some more bread," Madge said. "Fill the man's cup there, Sadie. More cake, George?"

George ate everything he was offered and kept saying everything was lovely and when the last cup of tea had been drained he asked Sadie to come and look at the flat above the shop with him.

"Ah no, George," she said, and backed towards the kitchen. "There's too much to do - "

"Go on," Madge said. "Off you go. Can't I tidy up? I'm not helpless, am I? Us old people are useful too, isn't that right, George?"

George agreed with her and offered Sadie his arm. She went with him although she knew the dishes would be sitting waiting for her when she came home and Madge would have had another couple of gins and she`d still have to make her a fry too.

George put the key in the hall door beside the shop and stood back to let Sadie in first.

"It's up the stairs," he said.

There was a strange smell, the smell of somebody else's house. Sadie held the banister and then let go of its stickiness. It would take her a month to clean the place, she thought. She stood in the middle of the living-room and looked at the fawn-coloured floor and the fawn-coloured chairs and walls and the photographs of George's family.

"Will you sit down, Sadie," George asked.

Sadie looked at the couch before she sat on it and George sat down close beside her.

"Could you live here, Sadie? With me? What do you say? Will we set a date?"

Sadie couldn't speak. She hardly knew how she had got herself into this position. She remembered the first night when George had asked her to go for a walk, and after that it had seemed impossible to stop. And she didn't want to stop really . . . only . . .

She clasped her hands together and nodded once. And then George leaned over and kissed her hard and his hand clamped onto her leg. Sadie let out a squeak and got up, pretending to look at the photographs. George laughed and slapped his two knees.

"You're the very best," he said, "you're a great, wee girl. Look around, Sadie. You can do what you like with the place, make whatever changes you like. I`ve done a lot of work already, replaced all the tiling myself, so I did."

He got up and led the way to the white bathroom. Sadie stood inside the door and looked at the new electric shower. There was a smell of plaster. George patted everything, the bath, the shiny taps, the cistern, the shelf beneath the mirror.

Sadie put a hand to her forehead. Impossible to think of being here with him, to stand here in her nightdress and clean her teeth and George in his pyjamas - waiting for her to get into the bed - no! no! She wanted to go home, to tell George she had changed her mind, but he had his arm around her, squeezing her shoulder, saying he'd look after her, and her mother.

*

Sadie sat in front of the mirror in the hotel bedroom and checked her make-up again. Behind her on the bed her wedding-dress lay discarded. She felt too hot in the navy dress but she could leave off the jacket. Hannah had straightened her hair for her but already she could see a few kinks. She didn't want to move, to leave the room and go downstairs again. Her uncle wouldn't leave her alone. It was his duty, he kept saying, in the sad absence of her father.

"Oh, God, I'm a sight," Sadie said to her reflection.

She put her hands to her face and closed her eyes, feeling the heat of tears, and when there was a knock at the door she leapt up to open it; she knew it would be Hannah.

"Are you ready?" Hannah said. "You should see George down there, everybody shaking his hand. He can't stop smiling . . . Are you all right? Sadie, are you crying? What is it? Having regrets already? Ha-ha!"

"Hannah, I'm scared," Sadie burst out.

"Of George? Are you joking? Sure, he's a pet - "

"No, not George, not exactly . . . Hannah, I never told anyone, and don't laugh, I know you think I did but I've never done it, I only let on I did. I'm still a virgin. Oh Hannah, what's wrong with me? I just never . . . I just . . . I was always afraid, what's wrong with me, Hannah?"

"Ah, don`t be crying, there`s nothing wrong with you at all. You`ve got the jitters. Look, it`s only sex, you know. It`s been around for millions of years, since time began, forever. You`ll like it, you'll be grand."

"George tried a few times but I always stopped him. He's so good, so patient, but I wish he had tried harder, it would be over me now."

Hannah pulled tissues from a box on the dressing-table.

38

"Is that mascara waterproof?" she said, laughing, dabbing at Sadie's eyes.

"Lookit, I'd change places with you any time, Sadie - heading off to Lanzarote with your husband! And George will be good to you, he's a kind man. Look at poor, old me, carrying on with a married man. I'm a bit on the side, that's what I am. You wouldn`t like that now, would you?"

Hannah laughed again.

Come on," she said. "I was sent up here to get you. The taxi`s waiting. You don't want to miss your plane. You'd have to spend your first night over the beefsteak and the lamb's liver!"

"Oh, Hannah!"

Sadie tried a laugh. She stood up and lifted her jacket.

"You look terrific, Sadie, you really do and your outfit's lovely, so it is."

Hannah held out her arms and they hugged for a minute and then Hannah went down the stairs in front of her calling out:

"Here comes the bride!"

Everyone clapped and cheered when she came down and said she looked gorgeous and called her Mrs MacBride, and Madge pretended to cry a bit when she got into the taxi. In the plane George leaned close beside her and Sadie tried to be herself but her arms and legs moved stiffly and she was hot and cold by turns.

It was late when they arrived and they couldn`t see much but Sadie was aware of the sea and dark hills and the air was warm. They had dinner in the hotel - George said the meat wasn't up to much. Sadie`s head ached. She looked across the table at the sweat on George's face, at the hairs poking up from the front of his shirt and she thought of his feet inside the polished brown shoes. She tried to drink a Bacardi and coke but she thought she would be sick.

When George was finished his dinner she said she wanted to go upstairs and George said he'd follow her up.

Confetti fluttered out of the folds of her nightdress. Hannah did that, she thought, and felt such a longing to be back in the pub drinking wine with Hannah and nothing to worry about.

She took off her make-up and cleaned her teeth and got into the double bed. The sheets were cold. She wondered how long it would be before George came up. Maybe if she pretended to be asleep he'd leave her alone. And then she thought that George must be shy too. Well, of course he must be! Why wouldn't he be? He'd been shy about everything all his life. Sadie relaxed into the white bed. She felt fond of him again and sure of herself. She would be grand.

George came in and he wasn't shy at all. He stripped, got into the bed and smashed through Sadie's hymen as if Sadie wasn't there. His chest rose and fell above her; it was soft and white and smelt of baby-powder. Sadie saw his wide eyes and mouth. A string of saliva swung towards her cheek and then George gave a great whoosh of breath and rolled over.

Sadie lay without moving, afraid to move in case her body broke up and fell to pieces. She knew she must have bled and the blood would be mixed up with what came out of him and it was all down there messing the sheet. So that's it, she said to herself, that's it. She smelled a new, hot smell and turned her head to one side, tears running into her ear.

In the morning Sadie said she was tired and George went down to breakfast on his own. She got up then, easing her legs out of the bed, holding onto the bedpost. She stared at the stains on the sheet and then went into the bathroom.

George stood up when she came downstairs and got rolls and coffee for her. He held her hand and kissed her cheek and during the day she began to feel better. It was lovely to sit on the beach in the hot sun, and to walk around the shops thinking about what to buy for Madge and Hannah. And George was very sweet and very gentle and told her she was precious.

By dinner time she was fond of him again. She ordered steak and chips, and when the waiter asked her if she'd like a drink, she said:

"I`ll have a large red wine, please."

George beamed and squeezed her knee; he said that she was a great, wee girl and told the waiter to bring the bottle.

Rosemary

Rosemary sat on the damp rocks and watched the tide come in. There was seaweed caught there, coming to life again with the rush of water. The sand was wet and cold beneath her feet and she rubbed her bunions together to ease them. Long strands of greying hair whipped around her face, and the letter in her hand fluttered. She turned her back to the wind and held the letter still. A bloody letter, she thought grimly, could she not learn to email like everybody else?

I'm sure you'll be glad of the company, Vera had written. Stuck on your own up there in that cold place. I suppose we should have spent more time together over the years but it was always hard to get away. The children have gone back to their own homes now and I'm finding the days long. I thought I would just stay for a week or two and see how we get on. I need a rest after the funeral and I thought you looked a bit lost and lonely yourself. At our age a bit of company is nice. And we are sisters after all . . .

Rosemary twisted and twisted the pages together and flung the letter towards the sea. A seagull cried and swooped for it.

"No nourishment in that!" she shouted at the bird.

She curled her toes into the sand and stood with her head down. Wait till Dominic hears this, she thought. I don't know what he'll make of her.

*

Rosemary always made Dominic wait outside the door until she was in the bed. He could feel the slackness in her thighs and arms; he didn't have to look at it as well.

"Come in," she called when she was ready.

Dominic bounced into the room half-undressed and dropped his shoes.

"Wait now," he said, and brought in a bottle of red wine and two glasses.

"I'd have been here sooner but only young Andy, you know Andy, he gives me a hand sometimes for a bit of dosh . . . ah, that's the best sound in the world," he said as the wine gurgled into the glasses.

"So, himself and another young fella stopped me going in to the shop. Booze, they wanted, trying to talk me into getting it for them. Well, I gave them a good telling off but sure they'd hardly listen to me - look like babies, the pair of them, skinny, wee feckers. A good feed would suit them - "

"Did you shower before you came over?" Rosemary interrupted him, sniffing at his shoulder.

"I can still smell fish."

"Well I did, Rosie." Dominic got in beside her, wrapping himself in the duvet. "But the water wasn't all that hot. Sure what harm is a smell of fish?"

"No harm, I suppose, but I don't want to be covered with fish scales. I'm not a feckin' mermaid."

"God, Rosie, you're a cruel woman sometimes. The smell of fish is a grand honest-to-God smell attached to a man going about the business of survival. Drink up now," he said. "That will warm and sweeten you."

"Thanks."

Rosemary took a drink.

"Dominic," she said. "I won't be able to see you for a while."

"Oh?" Dominic took Rosemary's hand. "What is it, Rosie, my pet, my dear? Tell your old man."

"Oh, it's all right, nothing tragic - just - I got a letter from Vera this morning, a letter if you don't mind. You know her husband died - the horrible Tony. I went to the funeral, remember? She wants to come and stay for a while. She thinks I'm fading away from loneliness."

"Well you're not." Dominic squeezed her hand. "You've got me."

"I couldn't tell *her* that. She'd have a heart attack."

Rosemary took a long drink and caught her breath.

"You don't know what she's like. It's a miracle she ever got herself pregnant . . . she said for a week or two but that could mean anything."

"Well, sure, well - will we not meet at all then?"

44

"I don't know. I don't know what it'll be like with someone here. Could you not get rid of your landlady now and again?"

"Ha! Might as well try to get rid of - of - barnacles on an old boat.

They were quiet for a minute and Dominic topped up their glasses.

"What's the woman like anyway?" he said. "Not like you by the sound of it."

"She's neat and tidy and she wears shoes all the time. God, Dominic, I don't know why she wants to stay with me - we never got on - and I've an awful feeling she's thinking of something permanent."

Rosemary leaned over and set her glass on the locker.

"Right," she said. "I'm not going to think about her."

She put her arms around Dominic.

"It's getting late - are you not ready for action yet?"

"Now, Rosie, don't be rushing your old man. Didn't I take my cod liver oil this morning? Will I stay the night? We could stock up for the few weeks!"

*

Rosemary got up early and made an effort to clean the house but nothing looked really done - she seemed to keep missing bits. She kept one eye on the clock and tried to wash up quickly but food was dried onto the plates and she struggled with it. For a minute she could see Vera, the child, standing on a chair beside their mother at the sink and sneering sideways at Rosemary with her sandy feet.

She abandoned the plates to the hot water and went upstairs to the spare room, which wasn't really spare any more since she had turned it into her office. She collected books and papers and her laptop and dumped them in a corner of her own bedroom and when the taxi arrived she was calmer.

Her sister climbed stiffly out of the car and Rosemary recognised Vera's slow, rising, poor-me pout as the driver set down two cases. She tried to smile a welcome.

"My dear," Vera said quietly with her head on Rosemary's shoulder. "How good you are to have me."

Rosemary straightened up and turned from the sharp, lemony smell of deodorant. She tried to dislodge the head.

"Nonsense," she said. "Wouldn't you do the same for me?"

Vera stepped around the cases and Rosemary picked up the smaller one.

"Well indeed I would, my dear - if you had ever married. You can't imagine what it's like to lose someone so dear, so close . . . I feel it, oh, I feel it. And now with the children gone again it's very hard to be alone. I don't mean to say that you're not lonely too, of course you are, naturally you are, but you must be used to it."

She dabbed at her face with a tissue and then looked around.

"Well, here we are, and you still have Granny's old things. I don't know when I was here last. When was it, Rosemary?"

"I think it was - "

"She was very fond of me always. Dear Granny."

Vera sat in Rosemary's chair.

"She'd be glad to know I'm here now where I'm comfortable."

"Come on upstairs and rest, Vera. You're in our old holiday room."

"Oh, that quaint little room with the sloping ceiling! Is it still the same?"

Vera followed her sister slowly up the narrow staircase, smiling and patting at the banister. Rosemary elbowed the door open and dropped the case on the bed.

"Shit!" she said and drew back from the puff of dust.

Vera didn't notice. She was at the window, tugging at the catch.

"I'm sure the sea air will be good for me only it's always so cold here."

Rosemary closed her eyes and tried to breathe evenly.

"I'll put the kettle on," she said. "Or - would you like a brandy?"

"Oh no, no, oh no, I never touch the stuff. My insides are much too sensitive. No, dear, tea would be lovely."

The kettle hummed in the kitchen and Rosemary eyed the brandy bottle, wondering if she should have a quick one herself, and then the back door opened and she turned to see Dominic's grinning face.

"Well? I saw the taxi, I just nipped in for a minute. How's -"

"Don't ask. She wants tea. Her insides can't take brandy. I'm not going to manage this, Dominic. She's already talking about Granny and -"

"Shh!" Dominic put a finger to his lips and pointed to the door.

There was a slow step on the stair and they waited for Vera to appear.

"I think the window's going to rattle," she began.

She stopped when she saw Dominic. Her lips puffed very slowly upwards and she stared at Rosemary.

"Vera, this is Dominic Byrne. Dominic, my sister, Vera,"

Dominic bent over Vera's hand.

"Sorry for your trouble," he said. "If there's anything . . . "

"Thank you," Vera said sadly. "There's another case in the hall there."

"Of course."

Dominic lugged the case towards the stairs.

"It's the room -"

"Yes," Dominic said. "I know where you are."

Rosemary rattled cups and saucers and avoided Vera's eye.

"He's a friend," she said. "I've known him for years. He fixes the - eh - "

"Oh, a handyman." Vera said.

"Very handy."

Rosemary poured tea.

"I don't know what I'd do without him."

She watched Vera sip at the tea. She could see her looking around the kitchen and she moved in front of the sink, still full of dishes. Dominic clattered back down the stairs and left quickly in the face of Vera's bent, silent head.

*

"Any sign of young Andy? He's supposed to come out with me today. Them young 'uns, they can't get out of their beds."

Rosemary was standing at the end of the pier. It was half-past six in the morning and only just beginning to get light. Dominic was getting the boat ready and it swung and creaked against the tide. There were other boats setting out and the men called to each other and seagulls cried around them.

"Didn't see a sign of him, wouldn't blame him . . . morning like this."

A drizzle of rain blew into her face from the dark sea. She clutched her old, white cardigan tighter and shivered.

"Here." Dominic threw a coat to her. "Put that round you. She must have said something. Has she no cat or a dog to go home to?"

"Smells of fish." Rosemary threw the coat back. "No, she hasn't said a word. She sits in my chair and lets me cook for her. I can't get my head to myself. Everywhere I go she's behind me, good job she wants her beauty sleep or she'd be right here. She wants to buy a television. She wants me to cut my hair and wear shoes. What am I going to do?"

"You'll just have to say it straight out, Rosie. And I might as well tell you, if you don't get rid of her soon, I'll have to pay a midnight visit to my landlady!"

Rosemary tried to laugh.

"She'd be thrilled, I suppose."

"She doesn't look too bad in the dark!"

Dominic bent and started the engine.

"All the same, Rosie, you know . . .   "

"I know. Come over to dinner tonight, will you? I can't spend another night on my own with her. Say you will, Dominic, I'm desperate."

"I will, of course, if you want."

The engine roared and the boat drew slowly away.

"Send her to bed early and we'll have the couch."

Rosemary shook her hair from her face and called after him.

"You have a good shower before you come near us."

Young Andy came to a stop behind her, his breath catching.

"Oh shit, I missed him!" he panted.

Rosemary looked at the thin, drooping shoulders, the tight jeans, the floppy hair. Poor, wee bugger, she thought.

"Never mind," she said, taking his arm. "There'll be other mornings."

*

Vera stood at the door with a growing pout.

"There's three steaks there, Rosemary."

"Dominic's coming over."

"Oh? Is that a good idea? The handyman? I hope he isn't a nuisance to you, you being a woman on your own, even at your age. Granny was only thinking of your good of course, leaving you the house, but you could have come to us at any time. I often said that to Tony, we mustn't forget Rosemary, all on her own up there. Well, there you are . . . if you've already asked him. He's a help to you and you're grateful I suppose."

"Vera." Rosemary looked straight at her sister. "I like being on my own."

"Well, of course you do, dear."

"And Dominic isn't a handyman. He has his own fishing business."

"Really? Is that so . . . ?"

Vera stood at the mirror touching her face and neck.

"What will I wear? You'll have to help me choose something to wear."

"It doesn't matter." Rosemary heeled potatoes into the sink. "I don't care and Dominic won't notice. He never does."

"You only think that, Rosemary. You've no experience of men, that's why. You'd be surprised what they notice."

Vera lifted high-lighted curls from her face and held them behind her ears.

"You didn't invite him for my sake, did you? Because I'm used to male company? It wouldn't do, Rosemary. What would people think if I started seeing some – "

"Vera! What are you saying? I didn't ask him for you. For God's sake! The notions you get. Wear anything, whatever's comfortable."

"That's where you always went wrong, you never made an effort. You always wore whatever you wanted, that eternal white, every stitch white. You have to dress up a bit. It makes men feel important if they think you went to a bit of trouble. Why don't you cut your hair? Hanging down like that at your age, all that grey. Put a colour in it. You could have been like me if you'd tried - you could have had a proper life."

"Jesus Christ!" Rosemary dropped the knife. "What would you know about a proper life? You had no life - everything for horrible Tony. What did you want for yourself? You don't even know!"

"What do you mean? What are you saying about my husband? He was a good man. I had what I wanted. I had a proper home, and children. Jealousy is a terrible thing, Rosemary."

"Jealous! Oh my God, this is too ridiculous. I'm not going to argue with you."

"It's all right, Rosemary."

Vera trailed a hand across her forehead.

"You're not used to company, people get odd when they live alone, I know you don't mean any harm."

She squeezed Rosemary's arm and smiled gently.

"I think I brought my blue, silk dress, it'll need pressed. I'll just go up and get it."

Rosemary looked up. Her eyes followed the footsteps across the room above and she gripped the taps until her fingers ached.

*

"Wouldn't it remind you of when we were young?"

Vera nodded at the candles burning in wine bottles. She turned to Dominic.

"We always used to do that when we were girls. Remember Rosemary?"

Rosemary sat across from Dominic and Vera sat between them at the head of the table. It was Rosemary's usual place but Vera sat down first. Candle-grease dripped down the bottles and there was a smell of garlic mixed with Vera's sharp, lemony scent. Rosemary didn't like the look on Dominic's face. He had almost bowed to Vera when she held her hand out to him. She was wearing the blue, silk dress and her hair still bore the faint trace of rollers. Her lipstick was pink.

"What do you do with yourself here, Dominic?" she asked. "How do you fill the long, winter evenings?"

Dominic glanced at Rosemary.

"Well, I'll tell you," he said. "There's not much to do. I - eh - well, there's the pub of course, and I read the papers, and there's always the television."

Vera nodded in sympathy, looking sideways at Rosemary, and said she liked the television herself. She began to talk about when her children had all been at home and Tony had been alive, and every now and then she managed to swallow a sob. Dominic's steak cooled and Rosemary tapped his plate.

"Eat up," she said.

"I am, I am," he said.

"And of course Tony loved a bit of music," Vera was saying. "What about you, Dominic?"

"Well, I do, Missus. I always liked the Country and Western. And do you know what? I wouldn't mind having a go at that line-dancing. There used to be a class here in the evenings but I never went. Friends in low places - eh?"

And he stood up and hummed and swung out his legs, hands on hips. Rosemary stared at his backside in the drooping corduroy trousers and Vera laughed and clapped her hands. Dominic sat down, red-faced and smiling.

"I hear you have a fishing business," Vera said, leaning towards him.

"That's right." Dominic abandoned the steak again. "I have. It's not a bad living - when I catch fish, that is. I don't catch all that many. I'm inclined to take it easy, but sure I've only myself to see to and the boat is my own. Are you familiar with boats, Missus?"

"Vera, please."

Dominic inclined his head to her.

"Vera," he said.

Rosemary emptied her glass and poured more wine.

"No, I've never been on a boat." Vera shook her head with a quick laugh.

"Would you believe that now, Dominic? Never. I always fly when I'm travelling, but I'm sure your boat is lovely."

"Hah! Lovely!"

Vera turned her head briefly in her sister's direction.

"Oh, have you been on it, Rosemary?"

"I have not! You wouldn't catch me on that - contraption! You haven't seen it."

Vera dabbed at her face with a napkin.

"Well - it would be very nice for me to visit a boat but I'm sure Dominic is much too busy."

"No, no, not at all!"

Dominic's eyes shone at her.

"Would you like to see it? I could take you out round the bay. You'd have to wear something a bit more hardy though. I have some rain-gear - "

Vera laughed again:

"I'm sure Rosemary can find me something . . . "

She moved her hands round her pale, blue shoulders.

"Something . . . suitable."

Dominic looked at Rosemary. She smiled stiffly round the table and asked if they wanted dessert. She held herself together and waited, waited for them to eat up, to drink their coffee, for Dominic to catch himself on and go home. She saw him to the door and Vera stood right beside her, waving and calling goodnight.

"Do you want a hand with that washing-up?" Vera asked.

She lay back in Rosemary's chair with her shoes off. Rosemary shook her head and cleared the table. At least she could be alone in the kitchen. Damn Vera! Damn, blast and bugger her - the bitch! If anybody was going out in Dominic's boat it would be her, and she wasn't, so nobody was. He was flattered because Vera wanted to go, because she fussed over him, because she smiled and made big, sad eyes at him.

"He's really very nice, your friend, Dominic."

Vera was right behind her.

"Has he no family . . . or . . . "

"Separated!"

Rosemary banged out the plates.

"There's a daughter somewhere but he never talks about her."

"Ah, he's lonely, the cratur - all bottled up inside him - don't I know what it's like myself? And men find it so difficult to talk - you've no idea, Rosemary."

"He drinks!"

"Well, he didn't drink much tonight. You drank more than any of us."

"He goes on binges."

Rosemary wrung out the dishcloth and snapped it.

"He disappears for days with crates of the stuff - you should see him when he comes out again - looks like a madman - grey hair, grey face. And he always smells of fish. Did you not notice?"

Vera was staring wistfully into the sink.

"Poor, man," she said. "I understand him. No wonder he drinks. Company is what he needs. What will you give me to wear, Rosemary? Actually . . . I think maybe I'll go shopping in the morning - yes - I'd better get to sleep. Are you coming up?"

"In a minute - you go on. I'll just finish off here."

Rosemary stayed downstairs for an hour. She sat in her own chair with the towel still in her hands and she folded it over and over and over. After a while she nodded to herself. Yes! she thought. Just have to get the timing right. It's just a matter of timing . . .

*

Rosemary stood at the window and watched Vera leave. She was moving fast, the ends of her scarf streaming behind her. It would take her ages to shop; she'd be telling everyone who she was and why she wanted something smart in navy! Still, there weren't that many shops she could go to.

God! I hope Dominic's in, she thought. She leaned out the window and looked towards the sea, trying to work out if it was fishing weather. Not that it mattered; Dominic went out when he felt like it. She snatched up her phone, tapped his name and waited . . . he answered and Rosemary's grip relaxed.

"I'm alone," she said straight off. "Do you want to come over?"

"Where's Missus - Vera - where's Vera?"

"Shopping. Do you want to come over or not?"

"At this hour of the morning? Ah, Rosie, was seeing me last night too much for you? That was a lovely dinner, Rosie. And your sister seemed to like me all right, didn't she? And she wants to come out in my - what did you call it? Ah - my contraption! Well now, am I free or not? Wait till I see . . . "

Rosemary pressed her lips together, willed herself quiet.

"I'll be there in ten minutes," Dominic said.

She got into the bed. The sheets were cold and she wished he would hurry up. Ten minutes, he said, but that could mean twenty or thirty or forty even. Supposing the timing was all wrong? She couldn't keep him there all day.

"Come on to hell out of that, Dominic," she said aloud.

She was beginning to doze off when she heard the scrape and bang of the door. She sat up but there was only silence and after a few minutes, footsteps on the stairs, not

Dominic's. They were too light, and too slow and anyway Dominic always called out to her on his way up. Are you decent up there, he'd shout and she would laugh.

The door opened and Vera walked in, two shopping bags swinging at the end of her arm.

"Why are you back in bed? I knew you had too much wine last night. Wait till you see what I bought, shoes as well, deck-shoes!"

She set the bags on the dressing-table and started pulling out parcels.

"I met Dominic out there, on the step practically. I thought he was going to come in but he went off again."

"He was going to come in," Rosemary said. "I was waiting for him."

She pulled the duvet tight and her shoulders were pale against the pillows.

"What for?" Vera glanced up from her parcels.

"What do you think? We thought you'd be all day at the shops. We haven't had a good fuck since you arrived."

Vera stopped pulling at the tissue paper. Her mouth and her eyes moved and her head turned slowly towards the bed. Rosemary flung one bare arm up behind her head.

Vera grabbed up her parcels and scuttled out of the room.

*

Rosemary could hear Vera moving around and knew she was packing. She got up and got dressed and she had coffee made and a plate of toast ready when Vera came down carrying a suitcase. She left it on the floor and went back upstairs for the other one.

"Do you want something to eat?" Rosemary said.

Vera looked briefly at the toast and shook her head.

"Will you ring a taxi?" she said. "I don't have the number."

Rosemary looked about for her phone. If she's not going to say anything else, neither am I, she thought. It's either nothing, or too much. They sat in silence and when the taxi came, they said good-bye quietly.

Rosemary went straight up to Vera's room. It was full of the sharp, lemony smell. She pulled the sheets off the bed and opened the window and then she stood on the landing and listened to the silence.

"God! It's great to be alone!" she said. "Nobody here but me," she sang out, doing a little dance step.

"No-body but me!"

Her old cardigan was hanging in the hall and she lifted it and went to the beach. The sun had come out and the rocks were warm and Rosemary paddled at the edge of the sea. Seaweed caught at her feet and the hem of her skirt was wet and covered with sand.

She wondered if Dominic would call in later. Would he realise she had planned for them to be caught? He might be annoyed about that. Well, she thought, he'll arrive or he won't. If he does that's good and if he doesn't, sure he can feck off.

Andy

There was sleet falling. It fell straight down in the windless, chill air but the boys ignored it. They were standing outside the pub hoping someone would lend them money or bring them out a few beers. Barney Madden ran them out of it but they went back when he took himself home. Like he owned the place, Stevie said, fuck him, all he does is wash the glasses.

Andy felt the unhappiness grow in his chest again. It was heavy and he fought against it. No, he said to himself. No. He held his arms up and out in front of him and made soft, crooning, engine noises.

"Definitely getting a bike, so I am, and it won't be long now. I'm still getting a couple of days on the boat with Dominic Byrne and he says he'll have more work in the Summer and I'll start saving then . . . "

Andy dropped his arms and sat on the wall.

"What do you say, Stevie Wonder?"

Stevie threw the butt of his cigarette on the ground and watched it roll into a puddle.

"I say you're full of shite, Andy. I wish there was more than tobacco in that fag, that's what I say . . . God, it's freezing."

They walked up and down, their fingers squeezed into the pockets of their jeans and their shoulders hunched and they thought about riding bikes on the straight, endless roads with the sun hot in the sky and their ipods loud in their ears.

"We're never going to have them bikes," Stevie said.

He nudged the rolled-up poster tucked under Andy's arm.

"That's as near a bike as we'll ever get . . . cost a fuckin' fortune even if you do have a job - most of them don't hardly pay more than the dole. And you've got Lily and wee Grace. Have we any fags left?"

Andy lit a cigarette and dragged on it before passing it to Stevie. Stevie had a part-time job delivering newspapers to shops. Great, he said it was, getting up at three in the morning, the streets all dark and no traffic so you could hear the sea, and then the day to yourself. He wanted Andy to come too when the other helper was off, but Lily wouldn't let him - said she'd be scared on her own at night, even though them birds were in the downstairs flat. She hated them birds; they were always laughing and talking so loud in the hall. Andy couldn't imagine their lives - he looked at them like they were on television.

The sleet began to fall thicker and faster. There was no one they knew coming or going and Andy could feel the cold going into his bones.

"I'm off home," he said. "It's too fuckin' cold to wait. See you later on, Stevie."

He pulled the sleeves of his jacket down over his knuckles and curled himself around the poster. One of his runners was letting in and he tried to bend his foot away from the wet spot. He went up the shore road at a half-run and paused as usual to spit into the sea; it was only a habit now; he never waited to see how far it went.

He stood outside the flat for a minute staring up at the window, trying to guess if Lily and the baby were in or not. He opened the front door and listened. There wasn't a sound, and then he heard a noise in the downstairs flat and the door swung open. Shite, Andy thought.

"Hi," he said, moving towards the stairs, mopping at the wet hair on his forehead.

The girls stopped at the sight of him. Their faces were bright and their blonde curls bounced on their woolly scarves.

"Hello! Hi! There's nobody up there."

"We'll make coffee for you if you like."

"We'll warm you up. You look like a wee icicle."

Andy bolted for the stairs.

"No thanks," he said. "They'll be home soon . . . I'll have to . . . "

He sniggered quietly to himself at the thought of what Lily might do if she came home and he was in there with them birds . . . they might have cooked him something and they'd have the heating on, probably had a big telly as well. Andy sighed, a long, painful sigh. He went into the kitchen and edged past the table to the kettle, batting the onions out of his way. They were strung from hooks in the ceiling. Lily had seen that once in a movie and insisted on stringing them up although she didn't eat onions - didn't cook anyway.

Water rattled into the kettle and Andy shivered with his hand on the cold tap. Maybe Lily would bring home something from the Chinese - she did that sometimes if her mother gave her some money.

In the bedroom he knelt on the floor and slowly unrolled the poster. The bike was red - shiny, roaring red except for the black wheels and handlebars. He weighed down the corners with Grace's bricks and then he looked at the wall to see where would he put it if he was let. But Lily wouldn't let him. He knew she wouldn't - she'd say it would frighten Grace.

Andy felt the heaviness creep up on him again. No, he said to himself. No. He sank onto the bed and closed his eyes. In a minute he'd get up and make tea and then he'd go out again. Everybody kept saying there were loads of jobs but he couldn't see himself frying chips or steering people round the dodgems. I'll try the boat yard again, he thought, although he couldn't see himself fixing boats either, and he didn't like those men, the Grimley brothers.

Andy's eyes flicked open and he raised his head. They were home - Jesus! She'd kill him! He stood up and pulled his sweatshirt straight. He scrubbed at his face with his fists. What'll I say? he thought. What`ll I say?

"Andy!"

"I'm in here, Lily - you just caught me - I came home to change my . . . "

66

Lily stood at the door with Grace on her hip. She was very pale and she was patting her face with a towel. She looked at him, at the poster still pinned to the floor with Grace's bricks and she pressed her lips tight together.

"There's a job," Andy started again. "Stevie was saying there's a job . . . "

He sat back on the bed, his hands smoothing the bedspread.

"Don't mention that eejit to me!"

Lily marched straight across the poster and leaned over him, Grace clutching at her neck.

"Get yourself a fuckin' job! Nobody's going to hand you one, Stevie or nobody else."

"Fuck sake, Lily!" Andy tried to stand up. "I'm going out now. I only came in to - "

"You only came in to lie down. That's all you do. You lie down and sleep and dream about fucking bikes, and your own child - your daughter . . . "

She thrust Grace onto his lap. The baby's eyes were red from the cold and she stared up into his face.

"We've no dinner," Lily said. "I was in the shop and I opened my purse – but there was nothing, there was - "

She began to cry; loud, angry wails.

"Ah, for fuck sake, Lily. Don't cry. Would you not ask your mother - "

Lily let out a louder wail. She hit the wall with her fist. Oh, Jesus, Andy thought, trying to breathe calmly. He pressed his feet against the floor and hugged Grace tight, trying to stop himself from jumping up and running out of the room.

His eyes fell on the poster; Lily was standing on a corner of it, wrinkling the smooth, shiny surface. He wanted to move her off it.

"I'll get a job today, Lily. Honest to God I will. I won't come home without one."

"Chrissake! What are you like?"

Lily blew her nose and slapped away the baby's reaching hands.

"Try the pub, couldn't you shift a few crates and wash glasses or something? Or Grimley's even, the boat yard?"

"I will, I was just thinking that very - "

"They're always hammering and sawing down there. Surely to God you could do *something*. And comb your hair - change your jeans. How would anybody give you a job?"

Andy put Grace into the cot. He ran down the stairs, out into the sharp, bitter air. The sleet had stopped but the sky was still low and dark. He pulled his sleeves down over his knuckles and wondered where Stevie was. He might have money for chips.

*

"You look dead beat, Andy - you look like shite."

Andy stood in Stevie's mother's kitchen and watched while Stevie poured boiling water over the noodles. The smell of beef curry rose, steaming hot.

Andy forked up the noodles and swallowed, feeling the heat hit his stomach.

"Thanks, Stevie," he said, gobbling and swallowing. "Jesus, I'm starving."

"It's Friday night," Stevie said.

"I know. Another Friday night and no fuckin' wages."

"You can come with me tonight, so you can. The other fella's buggered off down the country again. If I ask the boss he'll take you. He said he would, before."

"I know, Stevie, but Lily doesn't like being on her own at - "

"That's a load of me shite."

Stevie threw his carton into the sink.

"Does she want you to work or not? She'll be all right. Aren't them birds down the stairs if anything happens?"

Andy sucked up the end of his noodles and thought of flying round the dark streets in the back of the van and money in his pocket going home. Stevie gave him a cigarette and a cup of tea and they stood quiet in the kitchen looking out the window.

"You're a wonder, Stevie Wonder."

Andy flicked ash into the empty packet.

"I will go. Sure, feck it - she'll be glad when I come home with the money."

*

Andy walked quickly home with the plastic bags dangling, nearly cutting the tips of his fingers. He had spent most of the money and he had enough smokes for a week. Maybe they could have a few cans tonight. It was Saturday - a few cans would be good - yea - and a bit of decent hash and watch a movie or something on the telly, even if it was tiny.

He had the key in the front door when he heard the fighting inside. He could hear Lily's voice, loud. He set down the bags and closed his eyes for a second.

When he opened the door their faces turned to him. Lily was standing on the bottom step of the stairs, her arms tightly folded, her face red and twisted and wet-looking. The girls leaned against the wall, half-smiling. They started to laugh when he lifted in the bags.

"Here's the man of the house. Isn't he gorgeous?"

"Yea, just gorgeous. Come down here some night if you're - "

"Yous bitches! Yous fuckin' . . . "

Lily ran at them, her fists up and the girls shrieked and laughed and disappeared into their flat. Andy could still hear them laughing as he followed Lily up the stairs. She was crying; she hadn't even looked at the bags.

"Lily, Lily," he called and called her. "Look what I've got for us. Look!"

"Shut up! Shut the fuck up!"

"We can have a fry - chips as well."

Andy tumbled the packets onto the kitchen table. He tried to sound happy. He tried to smile but his limbs were heavy and he wanted to lie down. It didn't matter anyway. Nothing mattered. It was all shite.

"Them bitches," Lily said. "They said the baby woke them. Shut up!" she yelled as the whinging started in the bedroom. "And where the fuck were you?"

Grace cried out again and Lily whirled with a grim face striding into the other room. Andy reached a hand to the sausages and rashers and then let it fall. There was a cake too, a sponge with jam. He heard the slap and the sudden shriek and then he heard paper ripping - his poster! He moved quickly.

"Ah, Lily, ah, Jesus!"

He pulled at her hands but she pushed him back and went on ripping.

"I was working, Lily. I was - "

"You were out all night! And I was here on my own with them bitches banging the ceiling!"

She pushed the torn strips towards him.

"You can mind the fuckin' baby now, so you can. I've had enough."

It was very quiet when she left. Andy knew it was useless but he tried to put the red, shiny pieces together again. The edges were uneven and shredded. He felt the heat of tears and watched them drop. He lifted his arms up and out and made soft, crooning engine noises and then he rolled onto his side.

"Oh, God, oh, God," he said.

He began to doze but it was cold and the weight in his chest was like a stone. He became aware of small sounds. Grace had dropped her soother and was straining against the harness trying to reach it. Andy bent and kissed her head and undid the straps. He picked her up and held her tightly against his chest. Her bottom was wet, the clothes damp against his arm. He rocked her and smoothed her hair and touched the soft, hot cheek with his own. She breathed snuffily and relaxed and slept.

Andy laid her gently in the cot and covered her. He went to the kitchen and put the stool beneath the onions. The knots were tight and it took him a while to get them undone. They fell to the floor with a clatter. Andy climbed down and up again with the extension lead from the heater. He tied one end to the hook and the other around his neck and then he jumped.

Susan

Nothing, nothing, nothing, nothing. All day nothing -
again. The worst is when I think I feel something and I go
to check and there's nothing. Sometimes I convince myself
there's a trace of blood but it's no use. Niall is asleep
already. Look at him - the huge bulk of him in the bed, feet
pushing the sheet out at the bottom. I feel like whacking
him with something - big, oul lump, sleeping there like that
without a worry. You'd think he was dead, the way he
sleeps.

I thought I was going to scream at dinner today and
I was afraid I was going to be sick. Chops and cabbage.
What a strain meals are now, and me that always loved my
dinner. I don't know if it's because I'm pregnant - God!
Even to write that down - or because I'm so worried,
because I think I *might* be. I sat there thinking that if it was
real, if it was true - the cabbage would be good for me.

I looked out the window at the bits of an old boat
the men were working on and I looked at the cat sleeping
on the window-sill, the sun shining in through the yellow
curtains - everything so peaceful and normal, and all the
time I was hot and sick and sweating.

And to think that Matty doesn't know, has no idea
even. I wonder if he ever, ever thinks about it . . . about
me. Oh, Matty . . . There he sat across from me, eating

73

quickly, not looking up. I stared at his hands as they moved, gripping the knife and fork, lifting bread, drinking tea. Brown, wide, rough hands, not too clean. And I looked at the hairs on his arms, all lying in different directions like he'd been scratching them.

"Susan! What's wrong with you?"

Niall was leaning across the table.

"Susan!"

"What?" I said.

"You're mooning there in the heat. We're ready for the afters."

He gestured at their plates and I got up and poured custard over the stewed apple. The floor was slippy by the cooker and I steadied myself. If I fell, I wondered, would I have a miscarriage? Paul said, ah, when I put the plate in front of him. That's what he says in bed too, just before and after. Ah, he says. The thing is - it just could be his, couldn't it? It happens to other couples after years of trying. Suddenly - bang! There you were, pregnant.

They were eating their desert when there was a noise outside and I knew Bella had arrived. You'd think she'd no house of her own. Matty's as bad. Brother or no brother, it gets ridiculous sometimes. They just about sleep in their own house.

"It's only me."

She sang out the words as she pushed the door open. Jamie toddled in and she fluttered in behind him carrying the baby. She always says that when she arrives and I always want to say back - oh, it's only you.

"Well," she said, kicking the door shut. "I swear I lost half a stone on the way up. This fellow wouldn't walk for me. I had to carry the two of – Jamie - leave Auntie Susan alone. Matty, take him on your knee, will you?"

Such a flurry she causes every time, especially when she's pregnant. Everybody hopping, even Niall, and Matty putting cushions behind her back. And that lisp of hers - calling me Shoosan!

"Shoosan," she says. "I'll just put this fellow upstairs for a snooze. OK? Any dinner left? I'd no time to cook today. Where would I get the time to cook - I ask you - where?"

She looked at the men and laughed and they both stood up. Matty moved the table out a bit and Niall pulled a chair over. She smiled all around her and then went upstairs with the baby.

Jamie was calling, Da, and pulling at Matty's arm, waiting to be lifted. I put out a dinner for her, scraping my cabbage onto her plate. She'd eat anything she didn't have to cook herself -even for the poor children, fed out of jars, they were.

"Thanks a mill, Shoosan," she said when she came down again, settling her skirt about her on the chair and shaking back her long hair.

"Aren't you great?" she said to me although she looked at the men.

"What would we do without you? You're a mother to the whole lot of us. Jamie, put that down like a good child. Matty, would you look what he's doing? Would you pay a bit of attention to your son? Isn't he a holy terror?" she said as she ate the dinner.

I didn't know was she talking about Matty or Jamie. I leaned over and took the salt from Jamie' little fingers and I could feel the heat from Matty's arm. I willed him to look at me.

Please, Matty, I said in my head but I might as well have been invisible. It's never any different, never a look, never a word. Even that night, my party night, he didn't speak . . . Oh wait a minute, he did. Jesus, he said. One says, ah, the other, Jesus. Talkative, the pair of them!

I don't know why I think of it as a party when it was just the four of us, me doing all the cooking as usual and Bella saying, isn't Shoosan great?

Duck and roast potatoes and lemon meringue. I can't remember how anything tasted except the wine, red and strong. I go back to my birthday page sometimes and read it over but it seems like something I made up. I still only half believe it - yes, here it is, April the 8th . . .

April 8th 1.00 a.m.

Happy Birthday me! Happy??? I'm delirious!! - I'm sick!! - I'm mad!! I don't know how I feel . . . smart - yes, I feel smart, like I've fooled them all, like I've fixed Bella for pitying me. But I'm scared too. It was the drink of course, and my new green dress. I kept moving my knees to look at the shine on it. The men drank beer and Bella and I had the wine to ourselves. Bella served up the food although I'd

cooked it myself. She kept swinging her glass around and
spilling drops on the good tablecloth. I didn't say much but
I was lit up and I felt good. I knew Matty was staring at me
in the new green dress and I began to stare back. It was
like being sixteen again, staring at some boy down the
street and you knew he was going to ask you out.

After dinner Bella went to check on the boys and
Niall was dozing at the fire. I went to stand at the back
door to cool myself and then Matty was behind me,
standing close up against me. I turned to him and he pulled
me round the corner. God! It was over so quick I hardly
knew it happened. The front of my dress was rolled up
round my waist and I tried to see Matty's face in the dark.
My hands clutched his shoulders.

"Jesus!" he said.

And then he moved away from me and zipped up his
trousers. My back was sore from the rough stone of the
wall and I was sure my dress was creased. I shook it down
and I laughed. I was giddy with the wine and my head was
light and then suddenly - I just wanted to sleep. And I am
tired now - I feel like I could sleep for a week.

May 30th I.00 a.m.

These days I'm living inside a dream. I stand in the middle
of the floor, concentrating on my womb, listening almost.
Over and over I count the days on the calendar. I stand
sideways at the mirror and something beats in my throat,
rising from my chest and filling my head and I look at
myself and smile. I thought about driving out to Boots for a
test but I didn't feel up to it and I *know* anyway. I'd have
called into the pub to talk to Julia, or Jemima even in the

library, she's always practical and sensible but I couldn't imagine saying the words out loud.

Niall yelled at me today.

"Are you gone mad or what, standing there gormless with your mouth open?"

"Niall," I said, reaching for his hand. "Niall - do you mind not having children?"

He shook my hand off and snorted and I heard him saying, bloody women. God knows how he feels, looking at his brother's children, got so easy. He never says a word about it - he could be relieved for all I know. I don't know how he feels about anything. We live together; I look after him; I do the books for the business and I order supplies and I cook and clean for him and make him comfortable but we're like two trees in the same field, two stones in a ditch. His life is mending boats, and the weather, and what time's the next tide, and Matty of course, the famous Grimley brothers, the hard men. The Brothers Grimm; that's what people in the village call them.

I felt weak today and I gripped the back of a chair. I wanted to tell Niall that I was pregnant, that I was terrified. God, oh God, what'll l do? Look at him lying there in the bed with his feet sticking out the bottom of it and not a stir out of him.

June 7th I.00 a.m.

Sick every day. I can't eat anything except porridge. Niall thinks I have some sort of infection. He keeps saying it's a virus and I've to go to the doctor. He doesn't know what to do about me or say to me. The house is untidy, the wash-basket is full. He's fed-up, I think. I can't cook - the smell of hot food makes me vomit. I need to be out in the air a lot and I keep drinking water. Bella comes in to cook the dinner. The men don't like it although she tries. She wants me to go to the doctor too.

"Poor Shoosan," she says, pretending to feel my head to see if it's hot. "You'd better see the doctor. It's a sort of a flu, I'd say."

And I`d been afraid she would know straight away! It's insulting, really, that no one suspects the truth.

<u>June I8th I.00 a.m.</u>

I move around very quietly now. I don't want to hurt the baby - or maybe I'm afraid my period might still come. Niall is getting worse. He followed me all weekend, in and out of the house, hovering near me, watching, watching. But today I had the house to myself. I went down to the garden seat where the trees are. You can see the Marina from there and it was sunny and warm again. I watched the boats bobbing about and I could hear noises from the road but they had nothing to do with me. I was just sitting there, half-dozing - and then it came to me!

I sat up straight on the seat and laughed! I could have my baby and Niall would think it was his! Why wouldn't he? If it looked like Matty, then it looked like him too. Oh, I laughed to myself and I could feel strength bursting out of me, and then there was a rustle in the trees and Niall was bending over me. God - he'd put the sun out, the size of him. His face was miserable. I'd never seen him look like that before, like he wanted to cry. He took my hand.

"Susan," he said. "*Please* go to the doctor. If it's something . . . something not right, we're better to know. "

I nearly felt sorry for him. He thinks I'm going to die and what would he do for his dinner then? He looked like he cared but I don't trust that - he never showed any signs of it before. I got up and went back to the house with him and promised to go to the doctor. And I would go, it was time. I'll talk to Matty first though.

Actually, I don't have to talk to him. I don't have to tell him anything - but I want to. Hasn't he a right to know he's going to be a daddy again? Only Niall is always with him. If you see one, you see the other, and if I go to his house he'll think I want to see Bella and he'll leave. Well, it can't be impossible - I'll think of something.

June 22nd 1.00 a.m.

On Saturday I hung around the yard. The two of them were working as usual, their two heads bent together; bits of an engine lying about and them big sails sticking out of the garage. The sun was bright and I squinted my eyes and fanned my face.

"Oh, I am so hot," I said, standing near Matty.

"Go inside and sit down," Niall said. "It's cooler in the kitchen."

"Oh, I can't breathe in there," I said, and then I sank slowly to the ground.

"Susan !"

Niall fell to his knees beside me; he peered into my face and I asked him in a shaky voice to bring me a glass of water and he jumped up and ran into the house. The minute he was gone I sat up straight and spoke quickly.

"Matty," I said. I wanted to say, Matty darling, but I knew he'd be annoyed.

"Matty, I have to talk to you."

He looked at the gate as if he wanted to get away. I had a brief memory of my dress crushed up around my waist and I wanted to hold onto his shoulders again, but he made me angry too.

"What?" he barked at me out of the side of his mouth.

"I'm pregnant," I barked right back at him.

It was like I'd hit him. He stumbled away from me and his eyes were staring.

"You're looking at me now all right," I said.

And then Niall came rushing out with the water and said that now I had to go to the doctor but sure I'd an appointment made already. It was time.

<u>June 30th 1.00 a.m.</u>

When I went to the doctor he took one look at me and said yes. Well, that was no surprise. I decided to call in at the pub on the way home and tell Julia, I had to tell *somebody*, and maybe to have a large whiskey for myself but there was a funeral crowd in, one of the Maquires, and Julia was too busy to talk. Charlie raised his eyebrows when I asked for whiskey but he said nothing and I drank it very quickly. Outside I had to sit down on the window-sill - I thought I

81

was going to faint - but I was all right after a minute and sort of pleasantly numb.

I have learned to wake before Niall and eat a biscuit very slowly. That way I don't get sick and he doesn't fuss. He has begun to relax. I told him the doctor said I needed a tonic - I'll tell him the truth when I'm ready. He's waiting for me to start minding everybody again but I've no notion of it. Doing nothing is lovely.

I sat quiet like a cat for a few days and watched for another chance with Matty. It wasn't easy. He went round with a black face on him, gobbled his dinners and left. But one evening when Niall was out in the yard the baby started crying and Bella went upstairs. Of course Matty got up to go the minute Bella left the room but I called him back. He hissed at me when I caught his arm.

"Don't you start that talk again," he said.

"Don't worry, it's o.k." I said.

He seemed to sag and his face spread out with relief but then I shook my head and laughed. I held tight to his arm.

"Oh, I'm pregnant all right. I am. And you're the daddy."

"Don't you call me that,"

He snapped his arm out of my hand.

"It's nothing to do with me. I'm having nothing to do with - "

"Of course it's yours," I said. "What do you think? Six years we've been married, your brother and I, and nothing, not a whisper, not even a day late ever. "

"Jesus Christ!"

Matty laced his hands round his head and bent over.

"One mad minute and now this!"

I threw my arms around his waist but he pushed me away.

"Don't push me away, Matty," I said, trying to hold onto him.

"Nobody will know. It's perfect! No one will suspect anything and I will never, never say a word. Besides I think we might have another one as well, or maybe more. I don't know yet but I'm only thirty. "

His face went pure purple. He made for the door as if he was drunk but I ran in front of it and put out my hands to stop him.

"Bella will be thrilled," I said.

(She won't be though, she's used to having all the attention herself. She won't be one bit pleased.)

"And think how happy Niall will be. He'll spoil me and put cushions behind my back, and I won't bother you," I said. "Sure what's five minutes up against the wall every two or three years?"

Matty groaned and held his head with his hands again and I waited for him to shout at me or to run off.

When nothing happened I breathed out slow and quiet.
He'll be all right in a while - he'll get used to the idea.

I sat down and waited for Niall to come in from the
yard.

Dolly

Everything was all right until the day of Maguire's funeral.
It was in the middle of June and even early in the morning
it was hot. Dolly was out the back hanging up the washing
- sheets, it was - I remember how white they were in the
sun. They looked like they weighed nothing the way Dolly
bent and lifted and flung them across the line. She stood
there with the empty basket and I could see her smiling at
the rooster after the hens, and the black cat licking and
washing. She was nearly like a cat herself, only a great, big
strong one.

You'd never think she was my sister and me next
door to an invalid. Indeed there's days my poor oul feet
will hardly carry me. Her eyes were half-closed and she
was so still in the heat, and you knew there wasn't one
thought in her mind. You'd think she had nothing to do and
there were the rashers and sausages lined up beside the pan
and Denis' suit to be pressed.

"Dolly!" I roared out the window. "Shake yourself -
we have to eat, don't we?"

And we did have to eat. I knew those Maguires -
you'd be lucky to get a ham sandwich in their house. Dolly
was wearing one of my old flowery dresses and it was tight
as anything on her.

"You'd better wear my Summer coat, Doll," I told
her.

85

"Cover yourself up. I don't know where we got you, the size of you."

And then I saw tears in her eyes and I was sorry.

"Ah, you're a good girl," I said, "and you do what you're told. Don't be crying over the rashers now."

The bedroom door opened and Denis came out in his long-johns with a shirt hanging over them - you'd think he was married to both of us the way he goes about - and would he take those things off in the Summer? He would not. The smell of rashers was powerful and Dolly made tea in the big pot, and it was nice sitting there with the sun shining in through the door and we were all content.

When Dolly was washing up, we combed and polished and I brushed my black velour. I tried to fix Dolly's hair but the curls bounced away from the big yellow teeth of the comb so I gave it up. The pink coat was a bit short and tight on her but she smoothed it with her hands and smiled.

We got into the car at last and I remember the dust on the road and the heat. Everybody was at the Church and we stood around talking for a while. Some of the relations were crying and Dolly started to get upset so I was glad when the proceedings were over and we got away. Most of the cars drove straight to the house but others took a detour to the pub and Denis followed.

"It's only decent," they said when we got inside.

"Gives the family time to settle themselves, get their hats off."

It was dark in there with the light trying to shine through the high windows and there were long beams of dust which I avoided. The men stood at the bar and us women sat at the tables near the wall and watched Julia. There were rumours she was going to marry Charlie and her only a girl. We talked about who was at school with who, and when, and decided Charlie had to be a good forty-five anyway, but there you are, he'd be good to her I suppose and he'd be grateful, he'd get the pub.

Anyway, we kept our coats on and our feet together and waited for small gins. Except for Dolly - Dolly had cidona. Someone said we should go on to Maguire's and shoes were shuffled but no one actually moved. And it was then the damage was done. Barney Madden took out his mouth organ - and him supposed to be working - never does a tap if he can help it, the same man - and someone else had a fiddle and music started in the far corner and Dolly was over like a light.

It was the same at home in the kitchen - music on the radio or the TV and Dolly wouldn't lift a finger for you only stand there with her eyes closed, swaying and smiling.

And who was there as well only Ned Maguire - who should have gone home with his family - sitting on a stool playing the spoons. Dolly had never seen the like and she laughed out loud, and Ned Maguire saw her and he smiled and laughed with her, and when we got up to go, we had an awful job to get her out of there.

Well, after that, Dolly went out every night, and I passed no remarks at first because she often went for a walk when the hens were fed and that. But then I began to notice that the house wasn't so tidy any more, and the beds weren't made, and even in the middle of the day you'd find dishes in the sink and Dolly would be standing somewhere with her eyes half-closed. When she asked me could she have a phone, I got really suspicious; I said no, of course. And then, Carmel, one of the neighbours, stopped me in the shop.

"I`ve heard she's in there nearly every night," she said, "with that Ned Maguire. She plays the spoons and he sits beside her. He's that proud of her, so he is, and indeed they wait for her and the music doesn't start until she comes in."

Oh, I fell into a weakness when I heard that. I could just see the picture. Dolly with her big feet planted and her all pink and hot in the flowery dress but there was worse to come and I didn`t want to believe it only that Carmel one is so correct about everything and would hardly lie.

"She's had a taste of drink. Ned gives it to her and then he walks her home. You'd want to keep your eyes open there."

So I did keep my eye on Dolly but I didn't know what to do. She was over twenty-one. Oh, I wasn't able for the upset of it. I told Denis he'd have to do something but he just looked at me like I was raving. Dolly began to carry spoons around in her pocket and sometimes she'd take them out and run them across her fingers.

And then one night she was different. I only had to look at her and I knew - I *knew*. She kept smiling, looking sideways at me like she wanted to laugh. Her face was red and her eyes were shiny and she couldn't settle herself. Oh, I was scared then and my heart fluttered.

Denis was footering with the TV. His braces were hanging down and his bit of hair was scattered on his head. It seemed like an awful long time since him and I had red faces and shiny eyes and I could feel this feeling rising to my throat and I thought I was going to bawl. I knew I should talk to him about Dolly but I couldn't think of what words to say and I didn't think he'd care anyway.

Well, after that I lived in terror. I wanted to scream at Dolly but all I could do was check in the hot press to see if the necessaries were disappearing when they should. And it was when I was standing there one day that I got the idea. At first it scared me a bit, but the more I thought of it, the better it seemed. I nearly laughed out loud at the good of it. I knew Ned Maguire would be scrounging around the beach as usual, so when Dolly went to look for eggs, I put on my good coat and walked away quickly.

I nearly turned back when I saw how far out the tide was, and the wet sand and lumps of seaweed I'd have to cross in my good shoes, but Ned had seen me by then and I called out to him.

I was too warm in the coat and the wind blew a hot, fishy smell at me. Ned started pulling at his ear and he looked all round like he wanted to offer me a seat. I balanced on a couple of flat stones and smiled at him kindly.

"Ned," I said. "I'm sure you won't object if I do my duty."

"No, Missus," he said. "No, no."

He pulled furiously at his ear.

"Good," I said. "That's good. It's about Dolly, of course, my sister, my dear little sister."

"Yes."

Ned looked around for a chair again.

"You've been walking her home at night, I hear, and I'd like to know, Ned, what are your intentions?"

He looked straight at me then.

"Intentions?"

"Yes, Ned. Were you thinking of getting married?"

He tried a laugh but stopped when I went on staring at him.

"Married? Well, you know . . . if I could find a place to hang my hat - otherwise - I don't know. I don't find much to sell here, you know, and the dole isn't much."

He kicked at the pile of seaweed he had gathered up and shook his head.

"I'm sorry to hear that, Ned, because I have to tell you that Dolly - poor Dolly - finds herself in the family way."

I watched his face when I said it; he turned white as a clean sheet and then he turned bright red - I thought he was going to pass out.

"Ned," I said. "I don't want to lose Dolly and me next door to an invalid. She can stay with me and I'll look after her, and the best thing for you, Ned, would be to go straight up to Belfast and find work for yourself - right away. Now, you'll need a little something to get you started."

And I felt in the pocket of my good coat and drew out my cheque book and a pen, and Ned and I settled things between us very neatly.

That evening I felt almost sorry for Dolly when she left for the pub although I knew I had done the right thing. She would have got into trouble sometime and Ned would have gone off anyway. I'd be nice to her now, buy her a coat or a dress or a phone even. The evening passed and Denis came in for his supper. He watched the television for a while, and then he went off to bed and I waited for Dolly.

Her step was slower than usual. She came in heavily and sat down. There were tears in her eyes and on her cheeks.

"Are you all right, Dolly?" I asked her straight away.

"Is it that Ned Maguire? I heard he'd gone away to look for work. Don't you be crying, Doll. Aren't you happy here with me and Denis? I'll buy you a new coat, Dolly, like my Summer one, and a dress too if you like."

But the more I talked, the more she cried. She tried to smile but she couldn't so I sat beside her with a hanky and held her hand, and after a while I made her a cup of tea and sent her to bed. She'd forget him soon enough sure what was he only a waster who played the spoons in a pub! Dolly would be her old self again. The house would be tidy and clean and there'd be sheets hanging bright on the line and we'd all be happy.

But oh, when I got up in the morning - such a shock! I got up to a cold kitchen, no fire lighting, no rashers frying, and no Dolly. She was gone, the flowery dress was gone, my pink Summer coat was gone. Oh, I went into a terrible weakness and Denis would do nothing. She was a big girl, he said, and had gone off about her business. Gone to Belfast, I thought to myself, after Ned Maguire. But I said nothing.

A girl comes in from the village now, to wash and cook and that. She works hard and does what she's told. Mind you, I'm not saying I don't miss Dolly sometimes, because I do. She was a good girl, so she was . . . our Dolly . . .

Julia

Julia shot upright in the bed - wide awake. She listened, listened . . . and there was the noise again, like a footfall, a single step. She tried to speak, to scream!

"Is that you, Da?" she managed a whisper.

Her eyes lit on the door handle - she would see it turn and then the door would open and - Julia did scream then, swallowing back the sound. Have sense, she told herself. Old houses always creak at night - there are no ghosts - he will not come back. With a corner of the sheet she wiped her face and neck.

"Oh, God!" she whispered.

"I can't go on like this - every night, every night. There must be some way out."

Her fingers felt for her mother`s locket at her neck and she pressed it into her skin. She wanted to get up and make tea but the dark beyond the door kept her pinned to the bed. Outside, the Harp sign groaned in a sudden wind; the street-lamp flickered and threw a dim light into the room. Julia hated the cold, dead colour of it. She lay down again and closed her eyes, her arms crossed tightly.

And then there really was a noise. Charlie was in, sweeping up, cleaning ashtrays. In a minute the back door would bang as he went in and out to the store. The seagulls were up too. They screeched over the house and Julia relaxed; it was morning. She slept deeply for an hour and then the alarm went off. It was cold when she got up; the Summer was over.

Downstairs Charlie pushed the mop across the tiles and the familiar, hot smell of dettol rose to meet her.

"Nearly done," Charlie said with a wink.

His head shone with effort; a clean, white apron stretched over the fullness of his stomach and his runners left tracks on the wet floor. Julia stood on the boards behind the bar. The stools were all lined up and the counter shone with polish. Charlie was good that way, neat about his work, and careful. It was nice like this in the mornings, so clean and quiet and the early sun slanting across the floor. In half an hour they would open and she would smile and talk and listen and the night would be forgotten.

"Come up when you're ready," she said to Charlie, turning to the stairs again.

She puts eggs in the saucepan, bread under the grill and set the table. Charlie would be hungry - and there he was - his step loud on the stairs. Julia wet the tea.

"There you are now." Charlie hung up his apron and pulled down his jersey.

"Those crates of stout should be here this morning. Did you ring your man yesterday?"

"Yes. He said it wasn't his fault, he said he brought what Barney ordered."

"God, that Barney! He's getting worse, so he is, him and his godallmightys! Do you know what   he told me the other day, they had a visitation at his house, that's what he called it, a visitation. That day he got the half bottle of whiskey, some relation or other was arriving but him and Sarah drank it between them. What are they like at all? I know you don't want to let him go, Julia, on account of your father and all that and he's been here forever, but, well, I'll just see to the orders myself in future."

Julia nodded, not worrying. Charlie would sort it out. She leaned her chin on her hand, picking at the toast. If she closed her eyes she would fall asleep again, here in the warm, daytime kitchen.

"Are you all right, Julia?"

"Yes . . . "

"You look tired, child, are you sleeping? The strain of course, this last year . . . "

Julia wondered what Charlie would make of her panics at night. He'd think it was some sort of female thing, her nerves maybe.

"You don't look the best, Julia. I was thinking that lately - you don't look the best and that's a fact. I was thinking . . . "

Charlie moved his chair. He set down his spoon and smoothed his thinning hair and then he pulled the chair back in again.

"I was thinking . . . "

"What, Charlie? Is it a new drink you want to get in?"

"No, nothing like that . . . "

"Do you want time off? A week or two? You can go whenever you like now the Summer's over. Barney could do a few extra hours, give me a hand. You never take a break, you should go abroad somewhere, get some sunshine, a bit of heat."

"Ah, where would I go? And you're one to be talking, you never go away yourself."

"Well what is it, Charlie? Just say it."

"Well then, Julia. I've been working here a long time . . . "

Julia frowned. What could be wrong? He wasn't going to leave, was he? God! How would she manage? He licked his finger and dabbed at crumbs of toast and then he looked straight at her.

"This place, this pub - it's as much my life as yours - and I was thinking - you're only a young woman of course . . . I`m over forty myself and that's a fact, but you live so quiet here and . . . well your father's been dead a year now. So, Julia - what do you say we get married?"

Charlie sat back in his chair with a puff of breath. He stared at his plate, waiting, but Julia didn't speak and after a minute he leaned forward again.

"You see we'd be company. You shouldn`t be on your own here . . . and, maybe, Julia, only if you wanted of course - well, there might be a child - to come in for the pub. I mean - what's going to happen to it when we've gone? There's no one . . . "

You get up in the morning, Julia thought, and it's just another day, and then it's not just another day.

"Well." Charlie stood up awkwardly. "I'll leave you to think about it. It's only if you want. You'll need time to think - only natural - quiet girl like you."

He lifted his tea and drained it and Julia watched his throat move under the heavy chin.

"I'll open up," he said.

The tea cooled in Julia's cup; bits of sticky egg grew hard on the plates. There were noises downstairs, voices, doors banging. The first customers were in, sitting over early pints, reading their newspapers. Julia sat on at the table, not moving. She'd be able to sleep at night - that was the first clear thought - she wouldn't be frightened if Charlie was there. If she went to the pictures with Hannah and Sadie, he'd still be up when she came in. If she had a nightmare he'd be there when she woke up.

And nothing to stop her having a baby, more than one even. She'd be safe, secure, Charlie would be good to her, she knew that. And children growing up in here as she had done herself. They'd bring life back to these old rooms. She ran her fingers along the rough edge of the table - she had been five or six when she bit off all the varnish - she could still remember the flakes in her mouth and the dark, brown taste of it.

She thought of her last boyfriend, the laughs they had in his attic bedroom until he'd left for Canada. He'd asked her to go with him but she hadn't the courage to talk to her father about it. She hadn't laughed much since then, not since her father died for sure.

Slowly she moved the plates together and got up.

Julia tried to concentrate on giving change and reaching for the right bottle but it wasn't easy. The music in the corner distracted her and there was a crowd of lads in, a twenty first birthday party. She longed for closing time so she could think. Charlie had said no more to her; he was just his usual, kind self.

She looked up at a sudden shout - the Brothers Grimm, well on in drink as usual.

"Sell the bloody thing!" One of them roared. "I'm telling you to sell it!"

Julia looked at the two men. Their faces were fierce, their pints gripped in their fists; one of them banged the table.

"It's your only way out. Sell the damn thing."

Julia leaned suddenly against the sink. She held a glass under the running water until Charlie tapped her shoulder.

"Are you all right, Julia?"

"Charlie! I need - I want to go out for a bit. You can manage, can't you? Just for a while?"

"Yes, of course. But where are you going? Julia? Julia . . . "

The breeze and the salt smell of the sea were fresh after the heat and smoke of the bar. Julia stood and breathed in, feeling the sting of it. Then she turned up her collar and almost ran to the beach. It was a clear night with a bit of a moon and a few stars and the tide was in. There was no one about except for her old customer Arthur Swann, standing like a statue looking out to sea. I'm not the only one with problems, Julia half laughed to herself, a laugh with a sob behind it. And she thought of the Brothers Grimm and their shouted conversation.

Sell the place . . . I could sell up and leave . . . She walked slowly along the pebbled edge of the sea, lifting her face to the damp air. Why did I never even think of that? I never once thought of doing that, to get away from here . . .

She shivered, thinking of her father in his long, white apron, pulling a pint of stout, his face cold and closed. I'd have money, I could buy myself an apartment. I could travel . . . Or I could marry Charlie and be safe, here in my own place, where my friends are, raise a family.

The sand dampened her shoes and she stepped back from the waves, staring across the sea to the dim horizon.

*

It was late when Julia got home. She walked through the darkness of the bar and poured herself a small brandy.

The kitchen was dim in the cold, dead light of the street-lamp. Julia touched the bitten grooves on the edge of the table. She laughed - and then she heard the noise. She turned quickly. It was louder this time, and she was awake, not half-asleep. She squeezed her mother's locket between her fingers. Oh, God! And there it was again, like a footfall, a single step. He knows, she thought. He knows I want to sell - he'll be raging - he'll never let me - oh, God!

Her neck was cold as stone and the brandy burned in her stomach. She backed against the wall, her mouth and eyes strained open. The door knob began to turn. Julia's breath stopped. She wanted to cry out - to scream!

"Is that you, Da?" she whispered.

"Julia?"

Charlie pushed the door open.

"Julia? What's the matter? Did I frighten you? Ah, child I'm sorry. Sit down . . . "

He took Julia's arm and sat her down gently.

"I just came to see - I was worried when you didn't come back before closing."

"Oh, Charlie, I thought - I don't know what I thought . . . "

Julia leaned her head against him and the fear left her.

"There, now."

Charlie gently hugged her shoulder.

"There, now."

Siblings

The kitchen was too warm, and it was quiet except for Sarah's occasional tobacco cough and the rustling of thin white pages. Sarah read quickly, stopping sometimes to laugh silently, her shoulders shaking. A bluebottle buzzed in the heat and flew to the pile of dirt in the corner. Tea-leaves, eggshells, bits of porridge - Sarah no longer noticed them, no more than she noticed the thick oily grime on the shelves and window-sills, or the matted clumps of dust on the floor. Her thin hand stretched from the sticky sleeve of a black cardigan as she read and her skirt, once a pale grey, was patterned with dribbles of tea and porridge.

The sudden, small noise in the hall made her look up. She waited, listening for her brother's key, frowning, her eyes searching the floor and the walls and then she rose from the chair. Barney's pipe lay on the mantle-piece; she stuffed it with tobacco and lit it with the long matches he always used, and after puffing and coughing she opened the door and peered out into the hall.

The postcard was bright against the dark linoleum. It looked new and neat and strange beside the pile of old newspapers. Sarah's breathing filled the hall as she smoked faster. She bent awkwardly and picked it up, a picture of mountains and a lake. Her fingers trembled over the address. It was addressed to them all. To Barney and Martin and herself.

Sarah kept her eye on the door, listening for Barney but the only sound was the bluebottle buzzing in the corner. She sighed deeply, looked to the door, and then read the card but the words made no sense to her. She read them out in a loud whisper.

"Hello my dear cousins. Just a quick word to say I'll be back from overseas in a few days and I`d like to call and see you all on the 20th - I`ll be bringing my new wife!! I`ll keep all the news until I see you. Love and hugs, Richard."

"Bringing new wife . . . Richard," Sarah read again. "Oh, what does it mean?"

And then the front door opened and closed and Sarah subsided into her chair. Barney came in rubbing his hands together, bringing with him a taste of salty air and a whiff of beer and whiskey from the pub.

"Well then, Sarah," he said. "Is the porridge ready? What a morning we had, a crowd from the city, you should have seen them, down for some party or other. I never saw people so nice about themselves, looking at the chairs before they sat down, looking at the tables. What do they expect in a public house - polish and perfume? I don't know what the city pubs must be like. And Charlie hounding me to dry the glasses and bring up crates of beer, more beer every ten minutes."

Barney reached for his pipe.

"And that visiting priest, Father Monroe, was in again, he works at the hospital, likes his vodka, so he does, drinks it neat. That's how they do it overseas he says, none of your mixers destroying the good, clean taste of it he says."

"Barney," Sarah began. "Look - "

"Sarah! You've been smoking my pipe again! Haven't I told you? You can have your own if you like. I'll buy you one myself. You're the oddest cratur - worse than them quare ones this morning. Godallmighty I'm starving. Is the porridge not ready?"

He went to the cooker and tutted at the cold saucepan. The gas hissed and popped as he lit it.

"Barney . . . " Sarah tried again. "Barney - look . . . "

She flapped the card in his direction.

"What's that you have?"

Barney dragged on his pipe and took the card. He went to stand at the window and read silently. He lifted his head to look at Sarah, moved closer to the light and read again.

"Richard," he said at last. "Now which one was Richard?"

"Barney - what date is it today? It says he's coming on the 20th. When is the 20th? I thought somebody was dead. I was afraid to read it."

"Dead? Sure who would be dead? Who is there to be dead?"

The porridge began to bubble on the cooker. The bluebottle rose and buzzed and settled on the wall.

"Richard now . . . " Barney puffed out smoke.

"Barney, when is the 20th?"

"Eh? Oh eh - the 20th - sure that must be - well last Sunday was the 16th because the match was on and we lost by two points, so Monday, Tuesday, - so - sure the 20th is today. It's today. Godallmighty, Sarah - they're coming today!"

"But who, Barney! Who's coming!"

" . . . Richard - I can't remember any Richard.."

Barney scratched his chin with the pipe and swiped at the bluebottle. His tight brown suit seemed to grow tighter as he puffed, and on the cooker, smoke darkened over the porridge.

"Ha!" He pointed the pipe at Sarah. "It's Dicky bird for God's sake! Dicky! Do you mind, Sarah - the little fellow? Judy's boy. We used to play that game with him - two little dicky birds sat upon a wall - that's who it is. Married by God! What do you think of that? Two little dicky birds - one named Peter, one named Paul."

"Flyaway Peter, flyaway Paul," Sarah said. "We played it with bits of paper on our fingers. Judy was too old when she had that child, she wasn`t able for him . . . oh, what'll we do? What'll we do?"

"Where's Martin?"

"Out the back at the hens - what'll we tell him - oh I don't like this. He'll get all upset and then we'll get upset . . . oh . . . "

"Well." Barney turned in a circle. "Well, what time is it? Sure it's only lunchtime - Godallmighty, the porridge!"

He lifted the saucepan, sniffed, then drew back his head and coughed.

"Well, it'll do. I'm starving."

Sarah got up from the chair and took three bowls from the shelf.

"I can't eat, Barney, the shock of it! And what'll we tell Martin?"

"We'll eat first." Barney took off his jacket and sat to the table.

"Butter us a slice of bread there, girl, will you?"

Sarah wiped a knife on her skirt, then buttered bread for the three of them. The back door opened and immediately two brown hens stepped inside, squawked and stepped out again when Sarah threw a towel at them. Martin darted in, smiling, showing them the eggs cradled in his jersey.

"Good, good," Sarah and Barney said together, nodding at their brother.

They looked at each other as Martin carefully set the eggs in a bowl.

"For tea," he said. "Two each."

He sat down and ate porridge and bread and butter. Sarah poured strong tea and drank, watching Barney, waiting. Barney finished eating, wiped his mouth and felt in his jacket pocket for the card.

"Look at this," he smiled at Martin, waving it at him . "Do you know what this is? No you don't. Well, it's a postcard. A postcard, Martin. And do you know what it means?"

Martin watched the waving card, smiling because Barney was smiling. He shook his head.

"Well," Barney began. "Long ago, you don't remember maybe, there was a little boy used to come here to stay. A little cousin, he was, younger than all of us and we used to play with him and tell him stories."

Martin listened to Barney, staring into his face, frowning, concentrating, smiling and frowning.

"Well," Barney looked around for his pipe. "Well, he's going to come and visit us. Won't that be nice now?"

Martin's face began to quiver and squeeze.

"It's all right, Marty," Sarah said. "It's only Dicky bird - you won't mind Dicky bird."

Martin nodded and smiled but the tears began to roll and his nose began to drip. He sniffed and cried harder and then he got up and went to the couch and hid his face.

"He'll cry all day now," Sarah sighed loudly.

"Godallmighty," Barney looked at his watch.

"I`ll have to get back - I'll ask for the afternoon off - and - eh, we`ll . . . "

He waved his hand around at the floor, the dishes in the sink, the shovel filled with ashes on the hearth.

"We'll - eh - tidy up a bit - for Dicky bird - and food, Sarah! They`ll want to eat. Can you nip down to Higgins` - get ham and a loaf, and . . . a few apples, that should do."

He buttoned up his jacket with an effort and went out.

Martin was quieter now; his eyes began to close and his thumb went into his mouth. Sarah watched him without speaking. Her hand moved slowly towards her book; quietly she opened it. After a while the book slipped a little and Sarah's head fell back against the high frame of the chair. A hot, close, muggy silence filled the kitchen and the bluebottle was busy again over the fresh spits of burnt porridge.

*

"Godallmighty!" Barney slammed the door behind him.

"Look at the pair of them! Sarah! Will you look at the time?"

Sarah blinked and yawned as Barney gently shook Martin's shoulder.

"Come on, Marty," he said. "Time to eat in a minute. You'll be stiff lying there like that."

Martin got up, rubbing his neck and staring from Barney to Sarah.

"I got the eggs," he said. "Two each."

"You did, Marty. Of course you did. Sarah, it's three o'clock and - "

He glanced at Martin.

"Marty, go and wash you face and hands, will you? You're all . . . "

"Oh what'll we do?" Sarah wailed when he went out.

"We'll have to tidy up, girl. I mean - look at the place. Could you not have washed up the dishes or . . . "

He stared around, helplessly.

"And did you get the ham? I thought you'd have done something by now. Dicky bird said evening. What's evening? What time is evening? Six? Seven? Eight? And do you know what I thought of as well, they might want to use the new bathroom."

"But - " Sarah turned to the stairs. "But – oh . . . "

Barney moved quickly, went up and pushed at the stiff door of the bathroom. He heard Sarah coming up behind him and he pushed harder.

"There's something in here," he said.

"Push it, push it," Sarah said, pushing at his back.

And then the door gave way and they tumbled inside. Barney sniffed, raising his eyebrows at Sarah. The sink and toilet and bath were black with dust. Sarah touched a tap and quickly withdrew her hand.

"Here, look at this," Barney said.

In the corner behind the door was a roll of wallpaper, brown along the edges, black across the top, and sticky when Barney tried to open it.

"Do you mind, Sarah? Do you mind I bought that when we got this put in?"

"Well, they can't use it, so they can`t, and that's all about it."

Barney dusted his hands on his trousers.

"They'll have to use the downstairs like everybody else. It`s good enough for us, isn`t it?"

The door of Martin's room was shut and they could hear him sniffing and moaning.

"What'll we do about him?" Sarah nodded towards the door. "He's been crying since you left. I couldn't get a thing done with him like that."

"I'll give him a drop of whiskey maybe. Look."

Barney took a half-bottle from his pocket.

"I got it today - it'll come out of my wages - for Dicky bird, you know. Nobody can say we don't know how to treat our visitation. I'll give Marty a drop in hot water and he'll go asleep."

Sarah sighed and followed him downstairs.

"We'll have a drop ourselves, Sarah - what do you say? Sure isn't there plenty? Dicky bird won't want all of it."

Sarah filled the kettle, her eyes beginning to gleam.

"What about his wife? Bringing new wife, he said."

"Ah . . . young women don't drink whiskey. You should see some of the things they drink, you wouldn't credit it. Black Russians, Sambucas – looking for beans to float on top. Did you ever hear the like? Beans on a drink! Oh, you've no idea, girl. You wouldn't have a lemon about, would you?"

"A lemon?" Sarah looked vaguely around, opened cupboards on spilled sugar and tea-dust.

"Doesn't matter, doesn't matter. Get the sugar there. Here's Martin all washed up and clean. Look at him, Sarah - isn't he gorgeous?"

"Yes, gorgeous." Sarah had her head in the cupboard looking for glasses.

"Here they are," she said, giving each one a wipe with her skirt before she spooned in the sugar.

"I got the eggs," Martin said. "Two each."

"You did so," Barney smiled at him. "And we`re going to have them in a minute. Sit down, Marty. Sit down. Wait till you see what we have here - for big boys this is - whiskey."

"Whiskey," Martin repeated and sat down.

The kettle boiled and Barney put a spoon in each glass before he poured the water.

"This is the way now, do you see?"

Sarah watched closely as he measured in the whiskey and stirred. She lifted her glass and sniffed and then coughed as the hot sweet smell caught her breath. She sipped slowly and then let out a giggle.

"Go on, Martin," Barney said. "You're a big lad now, drink up."

"Here." Sarah held the back of his head and his hand and waited till he swallowed.

"Well." Barney put a match to his pipe. "Aren't we the fine ones with our drinks and our visitation? We'll finish this and then - "

A sudden whinge from Martin checked his talk.

"Ah now, Marty, it's all right. It's only Dicky bird - you won't mind him, sure he won't, Sarah?"

"Not a bit. He won't mind a bit. Give us a pull of your pipe, Barney."

She took the pipe from her brother and made Martin laugh, pretending to blow smoke at him. There was silence for a minute or two as they drank. Martin made little snuffling sounds and Sarah patted his hand.

"Now." Barney took off his jacket. "What`ll we do? I'll take out the ashes, Sarah, if you do the dishes and that. And Martin could - eh - what could Martin do?"

"He could . . . oh, there must be something . . . what about. the floor? Couldn't he sweep the floor?"

"He could of course. There's a brush somewhere . . . "

"It's . . . " Sarah sighed slowly. "It's . . . "

She puffed on Barney's pipe and looked over at the bottle beside the kettle. Barney followed her eye.

"Well," he laughed at her. "It's not over there, girl. I know what you're at now, I do. And Martin? Did you drink it all up? Well, I suppose if you both want another drink I'll have to oblige you. Sure isn't there plenty? Dicky bird mightn't want any at all you know."

Sarah smiled and began to sing. She sang a bit of 'Danny Boy' and Martin's head kept time.

"Get the mouth-organ, Barney."

"In a minute, I will in a minute."

He carried the brimming glasses back to the table and got the mouth organ and blew a few notes. Then he played `The Wild Colonial Boy` and Sarah and Martin sang together. And then Barney filled the glasses again.

Martin put his head down on the table and Barney looked at his watch.

"It's five o'clock, Sarah," he said. "Maybe we - "

And then a car pulled up outside.

"Godallmighty!" Barney steadied his glass on the table.

"Wheesht," he said as Sarah giggled.

They tip-toed across the room, one to each side of the window. The car was large and grey and the two front doors opened together. The man was tall and fair and wore a suit. The woman was dark; she wore a red coat. She came around the car and Barney and Sarah looked at the high heels and the shiny handbag. The man took her elbow and said something and then they knocked. Sarah let out another giggle and Barney shook his head at her to stop. Neither of them moved. The visitors knocked again, waited, then knocked louder. Barney and Sarah watched the street and the man and woman came back into view. They stared at the windows. The woman spoke; the man shook his head and then they turned back to the car.

"Two little dicky birds sat upon a wall," Barney began.

"One named Peter, one named Paul," Sarah said.

"Flyaway Peter, flyaway Paul," Barney said.

"Will we finish the bottle?" Sarah said.

Jemima

My name is Jemima Flynn. When I first read the story of
Cinderella the ugly sisters were called Jemima and
Belinda. This, as you can imagine, has affected me all my
life. Am I ugly? I don't know. I contemplate my reflection
but I can only see my own self. Eyes? Well it seems to me
that one is bigger than the other, only slightly of course,
but enough. Nose? It works well as a drainage pipe and
doubles as an air-duct. Lips? Hardly a Bardot pout there.
And yes, I know that comment dates me. Sometimes I
wonder if other people find me ugly but the truth is that
until I met Kevin I didn't care very much. There was
Eugene Curran of course - I was pure mad about him for a
while. I even curled my hair and bought a lipstick, but as
my mother always said, your miss is your mercy, and from
what I hear people say, she was right!

I was an only child - I think my parents tried it once
and didn't like it - an old joke but it always amuses me.
They were fond of religion and I was their little saint.
When I was very small, about six or seven, I read books
about Maria Goretti, and Jacinta who died at Fatima, and I
would pose in front of the mirror with a flower in my hand
and a look of piety on my face. My parents thought I
would be a nun; when other girls got ribbons and hair-clips
I got holy pictures and relics.

My job in the library required little in the way of
conversation, except for my old school friend, Theresa. She

was always good for a chat and a bit of gossip. Thrillers, she liked, the bloodier the better, you'd never think it to look at her, with her pale face and pale hair, no sign of blood lust there. It always amused me, trying to guess what people would like to read.

For a while I took note of how people reacted to me. Am I ugly, I wanted to ask them. They didn't scream or throw up their hands in horror when I spoke but they didn't smile at me either. I had seen people smile at pretty women; stand up, sit down, smile and nod at them.

Perhaps I should have been a nun as was expected of me. They'd have found me out though - I had given up religion for good when I was eleven.

My teacher at Primary School was Sr Anne. She would open the door in the morning and stand there, silent, surveying us, the only sound the gentle slap of the black ruler against the folds of her black habit. And there I was one day, sitting sideways at my desk - even then I was taller than everyone else.

"Come on now."

Sr Anne beamed ferociously at me.

"What do you think? If you and I and your friend, Theresa there, were in the middle of the jungle, about to be eaten by cannibals, could I hear your confessions in the absence of a priest?"

She lunged forward, leaning her bony fists on my desk, her face in its white frame breathing all over me. I stared at her hands, at the tiny hairs on her fingers. I had seen a film on telly where a ship's captain had married

Humphrey Bogart to Katherine Hepburn. They were in the middle of the ocean, not a priest in sight. The question began to make sense. I looked up at Sr Anne and noticed face powder in the creases round her eyes. She leaned nearer.

"Well?"

"Yes, you could," I said.

"No!" She shot up, triumphant. "No, I could not. I could not, Jemima Flynn. I'm surprised at you. Only a priest can hear confessions. Do you hear that, class? Only a priest can hear confessions."

"But . . . " I started to interrupt.

But I couldn't tell her about Humphrey Bogart.

At secondary school religion was a very serious matter. We studied Apologetics - interesting, but not compelling, not when nuns insisted on praying for good weather, ignoring the weather forecast. I had seen it myself - it was going to rain all over the Corpus Christi procession. Three nuns on the assembly hall stage leading two hundred girls in a prayer for good weather seemed to me nothing more than an exercise in crowd control. It was just the same, I thought, as ancient tribes doing rain-dances. But I never said so. It was impossible to say things like that to the sober-faced nuns. But surely they couldn't be serious. And if they weren't, what the hell were they up to?

*

Despite all that, religion pursued me. Theresa always ignored my protestations of disbelief. She'd ended

116

up with four sons, perpetually miserable and tired and always ready to cry. One day she returned from some place on up the coast somewhere - a retreat house, she said.

"Oh, Jemima, you can't imagine the peace I found there."

I thought of the four sons, and the husband eternally hidden behind a newspaper, and I could imagine it very well.

"And the lovely people I met there," she went on. "Arthur Foley for one, so thin, poor man. Do you know him? He's an alcoholic, you'd see him about the town, talking to himself. He's a bit odd but we all hugged him. And we prayed together and walked on the beach at dawn and I couldn't help crying but then they all gave me a hug too. It was lovely. Oh, give me a hug, Jemima."

And she draped herself across my chest and hugged me.

"Look what I brought you back," she said then, feeling around in her handbag.

"Now, Jemima, these beads have several blessings on them."

She pressed the purse gently into my hand. The leather was dark brown and silky. The beads inside were the same dark brown, made of polished wood, hard and shiny.

"I think I'll go home now," I said.

"Oh no, you must have coffee. And look, Jemima, a souvenir, from the café we went to every day."

117

She took a tiny sachet of sugar from behind the coffee jar.

"Did you pay for that?" I asked her.

"No."

She laughed nervously at my straight face.

"I just . . . "

"That's stealing, you know." I said.

I followed her as she moved about the kitchen.

"Were Adam and Eve black or white?"

"What?"

Theresa stopped and looked at me.

"They were white - weren't they? Of course they were white. What do you mean were they black or white?"

"Do you still believe the world was made in seven days?"

"Well . . . no . . . "

She pressed her back against the sink and looked up at the ceiling.

"Well," I went on, "if that bit isn't true, what makes you think any of it is true?"

Theresa stared at me without a word until I nearly felt sorry for her and then she laughed.

"God, Jemima, you're impossible."

*

I woke up and stared at my left hand. The splint was cream-coloured and it was attached to various needles and tubes. The needles and tubes seemed to be growing out of my skin. There was a machine of some sort beside the bed, and another above my head that beeped continuously - like the beep when they cut the bad language on television. I listened to it. Fuck, fuck, fuck, fuck . . . I moved my eyes as far as possible without moving my head. Something white detached itself from the wall -a nurse.

"You're going to be all right," she said.

She had thick fair hair and red cheeks. I moved then and discovered the pain in my head and she bent over me.

"Is it the pain? I'll give you something for it. You fell on the rocks round at the long bay, knocked yourself out. Good job the tide was out! If you can talk I need a few particulars."

I answered all her questions, trying to remember falling, and then I gave it up and went back to sleep. When I woke again the sun had moved across the room and I was starving. I lifted my left hand - the splint was gone. I moved my head cautiously - okay - not so bad, bearable. And there he was, sitting beside the bed. I stared and he looked back, smiling. He was wearing a white shirt and dark trousers. His hair was black, his skin tanned and lined; his eyes were grey.

"You're in the wrong room," I said. "I'm the ugly sister."

He peered at me and I was caught there, couldn't run.

"Cinderella was a wimp," he said, and laughed at my surprise.

"I'm Father Monroe, the hospital chaplain - well, only for a week or two but I'm here if you want to talk."

"But why? I'm not a . . . I'm not dying, you know."

"Of course," he said.

"You're fine. It's just - the sister had to look in your bag, for identification - there were rosary beads. She thought you might like a chat. You've no family I believe."

I gave a sudden snort of laughter and stopped when the pain in my head woke up again.

"Take it easy," he said, standing up. "Would you like a drink?"

There was a little sponge thing on a stick. He dipped it in water and pushed it into my mouth. I nodded my thanks. After a minute I looked at him again. He seemed patient, willing to sit there for hours. I wondered if I was uglier than usual and then I remembered he was a priest.

"You don't look like a priest," I said. "You're not wearing a collar."

"Ah well, you get out of the way of it, you know. I've been in South Africa for years. No one wears them out there."

"Tell me about Africa . . . "

I closed my eyes and listened to him talking. He told me how you had to walk slowly in the heat, how you couldn't imagine that heat here at home. And he talked about the Zulus he had made friends with, and how you had to shake hands with them three times so it took nearly half an hour to meet a dozen people. He laughed, leaning forward, inviting me to laugh with him. But I was nearly asleep.

"I'll come back tomorrow," he said.

In the morning I was much better, sitting up eating my breakfast, and the machines had stopped cursing. The chair was pushed against the wall and I wondered if he would come back. Every time the door opened I looked for him. There were nurses and more nurses; pulse, temperature, blood pressure . . .

"You'll be going home soon," they said.

"Well then," I said to myself, staring at the chair.

And then I woke from a doze and there he was, looking at me, smiling at me.

"What's your name?" I asked him.

"Kevin."

He looked clever - surely he didn't pray for good weather.

"Kevin," I said. "Were Adam and Eve black or white?"

"Well now," he said, and I held my breath.

"They were black of course - if they existed at all. Does theology interest you, Jemima?"

*

So that was the beginning, and here we are, Kevin and I, in the middle of the Zulus. We are surrounded by cows and turkeys and dogs. The dogs have pointed ears, like wolves. The days are hot, so hot we have to walk slowly. In the afternoons we lie in the heat and talk and drink white wine and vodka.

Am I ugly? I no longer think about it. Everyone smiles at me here. In the Indian bazaar I bought kaftans - purple, orange, emerald. They suit my spare shape and my sun-bleached hair. I have blossomed into technicolour and stride happily through the dusty days, a fine figure of a woman according to Kevin.

At weekends we go to the Anglican church to hear the Zulus singing and later we listen to them beat the drums, their own private ritual.

Enough religion for anyone, Kevin says.

Brigit

Brigit sniffed under her arms and flapped her elbows in the heat. She had the cloakroom to herself and she took her time at the mirror. She fluffed out her hair and lifted her chin to tighten the lines that crossed her neck. Why should it matter, she thought. He's the same age as me, but she knew that didn't count. He likes me anyway, she said to herself. He does - he does. There was a damp, shiny look to her face and she patted it with a tissue.

A door closed in the corridor and she looked at her watch and smiled. There he was! Oh, he was such a package; so safe and sure and solid. Maybe it would be today - it would - it must be. Brigit let out a long, trembly breath. He was coming in so often now, making excuses, pretending to look for things.

Sometimes, at night, when her parents were asleep and she was drinking her last glass of wine, she'd put down her book and imagine the two of them in her father's boat, like Grace Kelly and Bing Crosby in that old movie, and she would giggle to herself wondering if Brendan could sing. But sometimes she was afraid they would go on forever as they were now, skating around each other.

She stared into the mirror until her reflection dissolved and she could see Brendan at the door of her office:

She swivelled on her chair and smiled at him. He smiled back and sauntered over.

"Hi, Brigit," he said, sitting on the edge of her desk.

"Want to go out Friday night?"

He smoothed back his dark hair.

"We could catch a movie if you like, have some dinner – there's a little place I know down at the harbour. What do you say?"

Brigit held his gaze, still smiling and swung a little on the chair.

"Friday? I'm not sure about Friday. I think - no wait, that's Friday week - yes, all right Brendan, that would be lovely."

"I'll pick you up at seven-thirty," he said, standing up. "On the dot now. Don't keep me waiting, I know what you girls are like."

They both laughed and he waved from the door and went off down the corridor.

Brigit pressed her hands to her hot face. In the mirror her eyes were happy and shining and her face was pink. I look . . . radiant, she thought. Maybe it really, really would be today.

It was nearly time to go home when Brigit became aware of him standing at the door. She gripped the mouse tightly and tried to concentrate on the screen. The late sun slanted through her office and she could feel sweat gather; she wanted to sniff under her arms. She tapped on the keyboard and lines of figures ran up and up. Brigit fixed her eyes on them until she was dizzy. Jesus! She thought. Is he going to stand there all day or what?

"Eh - Brigit - are you busy? Could I have a quick word?"

She heard his step and then the loud, slow beat of her heart. Now, she thought, turn and smile, now.

"Yes?" She turned and smiled straight up at him.

He stood with his hands in his pockets, staring down at his feet and then he began to pace in front of her desk, back and forward through the slanted sun. Oh, you are such a package, Brigit thought. So sure and safe, safe as houses in your tight, tidy suit and your yellow tie.

"I've had an idea . . . " he began.

"I think - eh - I've had an idea about streamlining a few things. There's a few procedures we could tidy up."

Brigit knew she had stopped breathing.

"We might discuss it sometime . . . "

"Of course," Brigit said. "I'd be delighted - I mean - yes - when?"

"Well, I thought . . . maybe after work some evening, if that's all right . . . whatever day would . . . "

Brigit laughed. She moved the mouse across the mat and the screen changed. Under her arms sweat prickled and ran. Brendan took his hands from his pockets and pressed the tips of his fingers on her desk.

"Well," he said. "If - "

"Would Friday be all right?"

Brigit heard her own voice loud in her ears. She let go of the mouse and touched her throat. I shouldn't have laughed, she thought.

"Fine, yes, Friday's fine."

Brendan stepped back from the desk.

"It would be beneficial, I think. It's very good of you to take the time."

"No, no, that's ok. I'm sure you're right. There's things . . . "

She waved her hand at the desk.

"Yes, well . . . "

Brendan smoothed back his dark hair and moved towards the door.

"We'll get it sorted."

He half-lifted his hand in a sort of wave and then he was gone.

There was noise in the corridor; people talking, going home. Brigit sat still. She looked at the damp spots on the desk where his fingers had pressed and then she touched them one by one. Well, she thought. Well now. She got up quickly and went to the door - the corridor was empty. She stepped back into her office and gave a little skip.

"I've done it! He's done it! I have a date on Friday night!"

A date! A date! she thought. And he made up an excuse to ask me, and he was so serious. He was nervous - because of me! She moved suddenly to the window to see if he'd gone. His car wasn't there. When she knew him better they would go for drives in it, with the sunroof open and . . .

"Stop it, stop it," she said, fanning her hot face.

But she couldn't help it. And she couldn't help thinking there were plenty of women her age having their first babies - indeed, it was the fashion. Brigit pressed her hands to her heart and bent forward a little, rocking herself. And wait till they hear at home! They'll be so pleased . . . Ma'll tell me what to wear . . . she sat down with a flap of her skirt and stared at the computer screen until her mother's face beamed at her:

"A date pet! Well, what do you know! Isn't that grand. Sit down here and tell me the whole story. Oh, he's a cute one, that Brendan, isn't he? Mind you, I always thought you and he might - well now - what do you know! Reuben! Come in here - our Brigit has a date. Now, tell us word for word . . . "

*

Brigit hopped off the bus and half-ran up the road and into the supermarket. She was a bit late, her mother would be fussing, fretting over the dinner but the wine was running low and she wanted to celebrate tonight. And there was wee Sadie Hughes at the till, showing off her engagement ring, an emerald it was. I'd rather diamonds, she thought, smiling to herself.

Her next-door neighbour, Myrtle, was before her in the queue, staring round with her black eyes, moving so slowly like she was in a dream.

"Hello Myrtle, how are you?" Brigit said, smiling, feeling kindness for everyone rising inside her.

But Myrtle didn't answer, only nodded her head, dropping tins of cat food into her shopping bag, one by one, taking her time. Brigit sighed and tried to relax, to be patient, her heart beating with slow, heavy thumps.

She stopped outside the house, her hand on the gate, and wondered for a minute how much longer this place, this street, would be home, and then she saw her mother's face at the window and went in with a light heart.

"You're late," her mother said, accusing.

"I was beginning to worry. He's in a right humour tonight," she said, nodding towards the sitting room.

"There must be some crisis on - the government again I suppose."

Brigit looked in at her father. He was in his chair in front of the television, leaning forward with his mouth wide open. The floor around him was covered with newspapers.

"He's been shouting this half-hour," Bridie said, sticking a fork into the potatoes.

"How are you, pet? You're a bit flushed-looking. Everything all right?"

She coughed, turning her face from the pot.

"Get us my cough bottle there, will you? And just one of my little white pills. I feel I need it with your man roaring in there. Dinner's ready, champ and herrings straight off the boat. Are you starving?"

Brigit slowly took the medicine from the cupboard and then the glasses and the bottle of wine. She was dying to speak but she couldn't just say it straight out. She'd wait until they were at the table. And it might be easier after a drop of wine.

"I have a bit of news actually," she said then, unable to stop herself.

"Have you, dear? That's nice."

Bridie drained the potatoes.

"We'll hear it in a minute. Give us a hand here, will you, pet? And open the door there."

"Now," Bridie said when she went in.

"Turn that off, Reuben. It won't do your digestion any good. Do you hear me, Reuben! I'll pull the plug out on you, so I will. Get yourself over here this minute."

"Pile of shite anyway!"

Reuben flung down the remote control and kicked his way past the newspapers. Brigit took a mouthful of wine and swished it round her teeth. Her hands were damp and she wiped them on her skirt. I'll tell them very quietly, she thought. I'll be casual and . . . and cool.

"Well, look at you," Bridie said. "What's this news? Must be good with that look on your face. Reuben, our Brigit has news."

"Oh yes?" Reuben said. "Spit it out then."

"Oh . . . it's nothing really," Brigit said.

"It's just . . . well, you know Brendan along the corridor . . . oh really, it's nothing."

She shook out her napkin and smoothed and smoothed it on her knee. Her parents stared at her, her mother half-smiling, waiting for her to go on.

"Well, if it's nothing really," Reuben said. "Can I eat my dinner?"

"I have a date on Friday night," Brigit said, keeping her voice low.

She tilted her head and smiled at her parents in turn.

"A date?" Bridie said. "How do you mean?"

"What does she mean?" Reuben said to Bridie,.

"A date with Brendan," Brigit went on, her fingers digging into the napkin.

"In the office. You know, along the corridor - "

"Yes, we know who Brendan is," Bridie said, and her face was almost cross.

"But what's this date business? What do you mean?"

"He's asked me to go out with him," Brigit said, and her voice rose a little.

"On Friday night. He fancies me."

"That's nice," Reuben said, beginning to eat.

"Well, what do you know?" Bridie said, breathing loudly down her nose.

She stared at her daughter.

"Why all of a sudden, I wonder. Hasn't he known you for years? He's in that place as long as you are,"

"He likes me," Brigit said. "Lately he's been around more, and . . . "

"I'd be wary if I was you, Brigit. Very wary. Them quiet fellows . . . "

Bridie shook her head.

"You never know what they're thinking."

She lifted the salt and tapped the table with it.

"He has his own house, I suppose. And where does he live anyway? Where's his family from? Not from round here anyway."

Brigit felt cold inside in spite of the wine. She tried to hold on to the good feeling, but she could feel tears rising.

"He lives near Belfast - but he likes me, Ma, he fancies me, and I thought maybe some time we could take the boat out. I thought you`d be pleased for me, I thought you`d be glad."

"She is," Reuben said. "She's delighted, she's bloody well thrilled, I'm thrilled too. But no boat, the engine`s bust. The Brothers Grimm have it. Can we eat our dinner now?"

Brigit touched her mother's arm.

"Maybe I'll get married like other people. It would be lovely, it would be – "

"Married!" Bridie squealed.

Brigit lifted her napkin to cover the spilling tears and bent her head.

"For Christ's sake!" Reuben said. "Leave her alone. Why shouldn't the man like her? She's upset now."

"Upset!" Bridie turned sharply to her husband.

"She doesn't know what upset is. What do you want to get married for?" she said to Brigit.   "Aren't you comfortable here? You never said before you wanted to leave. Of course we're getting on now. You're bored with us, I suppose."

"Ma! Why would you say that? Don't - "

"Nothing for you here only knitting every night and listening to your father shouting at the television."

"You leave me out of it," Reuben said.

"Tears now and the dinner ruined. I know what you're at. Oh aye, up to your old tricks again."

"Am I talking to you? Am I? Am I talking to you?"

"Talking!" Reuben stood up.

"You're not talking, woman, you're ranting! Well, rant away. I'm going to eat in the kitchen."

"This house is yours," Bridie said, tugging at Brigit's hands.

"You have all the security you want right here. I don't understand why, all of a sudden, just because that fellow asks you out - "

"It's not just all of a sudden. He was always . . . there, you know. I thought you'd want me to get married. You did, you and Da - "

"Huh! Him? Sure what did I know? I was only a girl."

She put her hands on the table as if she was about to get up, and then she half-laughed.

"I married him because I liked his name."

"Aye!" Reuben pushed open the kitchen door.

"I heard that. And it's the only thing you ever liked about me."

He pointed at Brigit.

"Do you know what she said when you were born? She said that I," Reuben tapped his chest, "that I, was a monster to put her through all that, and she'd die before she'd let me near her again. One year I had of married life. There was no pills in them days - not that it would have made any difference to her. Marriage! Don't talk to me about marriage! Work, work, work for me - take, take, take for her. And I'll tell you more than that. She tried to make you the same as herself - wouldn't allow you as much as a lipstick - "

"Stop it!"

Bridie's chair scraped on the floor. Her face was flaming, her cheeks bulging.

"Ma!" Brigit cried out.

"You're a dirty man! Such things to say! You're a dirty man to talk like that in front of your daughter."

"Daughter!" Reuben roared. "Look at her! She's nearly a middle-aged woman!"

"Da!" Brigit clapped her hands over her ears.

"You have her the way she is. You turned her against every poor, pimply gobshite who came to the door. I remember all that. I knew what you were at, and here you are, at it again . . . ah, shite!"

The kitchen door swung behind him.

"Oh that man!"

Bridie started to cough and turned away. She tried to laugh but she was shaking and her face was still red. She pulled at her chair and sat down.

"Isn't he a holy terror? I swear he's getting worse. He should never have retired but there you are, they wouldn't keep him any longer."

She tidied as she spoke, coughing and thumping her chest. She moved the plates around, brushing at crumbs.

"There's people like him should never retire, work till they drop would suit them . . . I'll make tea in a minute."

Tea! Brigit thought. Her glass was empty. She wanted more wine - she was dying for more but the bottle was in the kitchen with her father. How could he talk like that, she thought. Or Ma either. I don't want to know about them. She felt like she was crying her eyes out but she knew her face was dry now.

"I was only trying to protect you," Bridie said suddenly.

"To save you . . . you have no idea what it's like - the whole messy business. I nearly died. It was horrible. I don't mean I didn't want - I mean I was always glad we had you."

She gripped Brigit's wrist.

"And you've been happy, pet, haven't you?"

Brigit couldn't answer. She shook her head. If her mother would only go to the kitchen and leave her alone. If she could just concentrate on Brendan . . . She stared at her empty glass until she could see him facing her in the boat on the blue water:

They were singing like Bing and Grace and Brendan was smiling, the breeze ruffling his smooth, dark hair. He reached across and took her hand.

"I've wasted so much time," he said. "We could have been doing this weeks ago, months ago, maybe even years ago."

"Everything has its own time," she said gently, pressing his fingers.

But she couldn't really see past the empty glass. There was a strong smell from the fish and the room was very warm. She eased her elbows away from her chest and turned her head away from the table.

"Well," Bridie said.

"Well, we can talk about it again later, if you like. All this food," she said, fussing at the plates. "Maybe later, we'll . . . "

She went across to her small table at the window and began to pull out the knitting. Reuben came in and turned on the television. He switched channels until he found the news and then he sat with a newspaper on his knee.

How could they say all that, Brigit thought. I almost wish Brendan hadn't said anything. Her eyes moved over the old patterned wallpaper and up to the stained ceiling and she felt the weight of the room around her. After a minute she got up and went to the kitchen. Her feet and legs were heavy and she moved slowly. She heard her father's voice ask a question. Her mother answered. There was plenty of wine left. Brigit got herself a clean glass and took the bottle upstairs to her room.

Myrtle

Myrtle studied the label on the tin. She didn't particularly like the cat's face only it was a nice, mustardy colour.

"Same as my coat."

A child stared at her when she spoke - a small girl with badges on her jacket. She stared at Myrtle and Myrtle stared back, leaning forward and making her eyes bigger until the child turned away, reaching for her father's hand.

"Recipe de Luxe," Myrtle read in a whisper. "Trout and Tuna."

That was a new one and it didn't say Trout and Tuna *flavour* - it said Trout and Tuna. She lifted two tins and went to the check-out. The man in front of her turned around and the child with the badges on her jacket was beside him.

"Not very quick are they? They must think we have all day to stand here."

Myrtle blinked away from his busy eyes.

"Yes," she said.

She clamped her teeth and lips together and looked at the man's feet, the thin legs in tight jeans.

"Da, what's wrong with that lady?" the child asked.

Someone moved in behind her and her shoulders twitched. She held the tins tightly, willing the queue forward.

Outside the sun shone, the sea so bright Myrtle had to squint. She walked home, stopping sometimes to lean against the railings, to watch the tide rushing in, to follow with her eyes the black mass of seaweed beneath the waves. She looked across to Carrickfergus. One of these days she would go - she would! She'd go on the bus and have a look round, and a cup of tea maybe, and she would talk to people, make friends . . .

"I wish I was," she sang, "in Carrick-fer-er-gus . . . "

And then she stopped; that was all she knew.

She went into the house, dropped the tins on the kitchen table and put the kettle on. It was a long time since breakfast. She adjusted the waistband of her tracksuit, rubbing at the red marks on her skin. She read the labels on the tins of cat food and wondered where to put them. There was hardly room to put them anywhere.

She had every flavour - Chicken, Rabbit, Veal, Beef, Veal and Beef, Chicken and Rabbit, Salmon with Crab. The tins covered the worktops; there were rows of them on the floor. She balanced the Trout and Tuna near the front because they were new. She stared at them until the kettle boiled.

In the sitting-room she sat with her feet to the radiator, warming them and drinking her tea. She stretched, leaning back in the chair, and wondered would she eat the doughnut or keep it for lunch. Ah . . . she'd have it. There was a frozen tart - she could have that for lunch. She bit into the doughnut with her eyes closed; her tongue poked at the jam and she grunted softly.

The car door slamming in the street made her climb slowly out of the chair. She gripped the edge of the curtain and stared at the sleek, black car, shiny with polish. A man with sleek, black, shiny hair stood beside it holding a small suitcase. Myrtle watched as he went to a door across the street, knocked and waited. May's house, May Toal she was called. She always wanted to chat and Myrtle had tried to chat back but all she could manage was yes and no and it might rain. May spoke so fast, jumping from one thing to the next . . . ah, there she was, holding the door half-open.

The man set down his case and opened it, then closed it as May shook her head. He went to the next house and the next, the drove to the top of the street and turned the car.

Myrtle watched him get out again. He would come here - knock on her door - expect her to talk. Well, she wouldn't - she wouldn't even answer the door. Just let him . . . no . . . wait! This was a chance - she could try at least. She could say hello, make friends with him.

She went in and out of the hall, waiting, listening . . . anyway, she wouldn't have to say much; he would do the talking: he was selling things. Myrtle looked into the mirror on the hall stand; when she smiled there were bumps on her cheeks. She lifted a hand to her hair; the long ponytail was untidy. Vaguely she patted the loose bits then went back to stand at the window. The car door banged again and there he was. He straightened the edges of his jacket, pushed the shiny hair down behind his ears, and then he smiled and walked up the steps.

The knock made her jump all the same. She wavered in the hall, wondering if he would knock again if she didn't answer, and then she moved quickly.

"Good morning, Madam, good morning. Isn't the day great?"

He lifted his head and sniffed deeply at the salty wind and smiled at Myrtle. His hair shone in the sunlight; his teeth glistened, shining at her. He seemed to have teeth everywhere. Myrtle stared, motionless.

"Could I interest you, Madam?"

He moved his right foot forward.

"Something for your pet?"

Swiftly he bent, set down the case and opened it.

"Does Madam have a pet? A little dog maybe, or a cat?"

"Cat . . . "

The word popped out of Myrtle's mouth.

"Wonderful. How nice - "

"No! I . . . No, I - I'm getting a cat . . . soon."

"A new arrival then! How exciting! Now let me see . . . "

He rummaged in the case.

"I don't seem . . . "

He shook his head.

"I have a lot of toys for dogs you know. I find these days most people have dogs, for the company - they like the company when they get on a bit - of course you're not . . ."

Myrtle stared at the top of his shining head as he lifted plastic bones and leather dog-leads.

"Very little for cats with me. They're so independent, as you know I'm sure, no interest in toys. What's this? Ah no, worm and flea powders - Madam won't be needing those."

He laughed and Myrtle shook her head. He moved his left foot forward.

"There's a new catalogue in the office - I could call tomorrow if that would suit - you could have a look. I'm sure there's cat-baskets, yes, and bells, door-flaps, all that. Would it be convenient?"

He whipped a business-card from his pocket.

"There you are."

He flourished it at Myrtle.

"That's my name there at the top -   Silas Bell. Mr Silas Bell, that's me."

He smiled and made a little bow.

"Until tomorrow, Madam. Same time suit you? It'll be a pleasure to see you again."

" . . . Yes," Myrtle said.

She clutched the card to her side, watched Silas Bell get into the shiny car, and then slowly closed the door. For long seconds she stood in the hall, staring at the letter-box. Minutes passed; her feet began to get cold. She lifted the card to read it again and breathed out noisily. She had talked, she had made a friend! Didn't he want to come back the next day? He had almost begged her to let him come back.

Myrtle ate a huge lunch and cut the apple-tart after. She was conscious of her new position as someone's friend and she felt virtuous, holy almost. She licked cream from a spoon and eased the waistband of her tracksuit, trying to think of names for cats and wondering what would be in the catalogue. Her fingers were sticky and she wiped them on a tissue.

She'd have a bath instead of a shower, she thought, a lovely, long hot bath. On the window-sill she found an old bath bomb. There was a smell of violets when she dropped it into the steaming water but it wouldn't dissolve. She poked at it with a toothbrush until it broke apart. Gingerly she sat down; such an expanse of skin. Her long, pale hair hung wet and straight, and then she remembered the rollers.

She dried quickly and tied her dressing-gown, but she couldn't find the rollers! Where were they? Where! Drawer after drawer was tumbled. Myrtle breathed with quick, loud, anxious gasps and spit ran across her chin. There! She had them! She divided her hair carefully into ten sections, rolled it around the curlers and snapped the elastic into place.

In the morning she was up early. Her head ached in ten places. She stared at the ringlets, pulled them down and watched them shoot back up again. She drew a hairbrush through them, gently over the sore spots. The tracksuit was dropped to the floor - it wouldn't do - wouldn't match the curls. There must be something - there'd be something in the spare-room - there was a box . . .

The black dress fitted very neatly; Myrtle held her breath to get the zip up. It was all right only she was cold. She put on her old lilac fleece - she could take it off when he arrived. The face in the mirror looked odd, not like her own face at all, and too pale against the dark dress. Lipstick! She should have lipstick, but . . . wasn't there a book with a hard, red cover . . . yes. She wet her finger and rubbed until the colour began to run, then pressed the colour to her lips. Well . . . it would do only she couldn't have a cup of tea now.

What time was it? He said, at the same time. She stood in front of the fire, trying not to lick her lips or bite them. Eleven, half-eleven, nearly twelve - and there he was, the shiny, black car coming to a stop outside her door. Silas Bell pushed his hair flat behind his ears, lifted his case from the back seat, and smiled.

"Well, here I am again as promised," he began when she opened the door.

He gaped at her, his mouth open; there was a glitter of teeth and then he went on:

"I've brought the catalogue."

He waved it in the air, smiling and sliding his right foot forward.

"Yes, Myrtle said."

He shivered suddenly and hunched his shoulder against the breeze.

"Maybe . . . "

Myrtle opened the door wider.

"Maybe, would . . . ?"

"Yes indeed, thank you. I would indeed."

Silas Bell followed Myrtle into the sitting-room; he opened his case and handed her the catalogue and set a laptop on the table.

"Fresh outside today, Madam," he said, sitting down when she did. "Bracing. Very warm in here though."

Myrtle turned the pages and the pictures slid past her eyes. She could feel him watching her.

"Page sixteen, Madam," he suggested.

"I thought, since you're getting a cat you might like a basket. There's a really nice wicker-work model, well lined with cotton. It's just the thing for cats these sharp nights. You can't be too - "

"Yes." Myrtle looked up at him. "A basket."

"Wonderful!"

Silas Bell opened his laptop and typed into it very quickly.

"You've made a good choice, madam. I thought you would like that one."

"Name?" he said, fingers poised.

"Oh - Smith - Myrtle Smith."

"Well now." Silas Bell beamed at her.

"My dearest aunt was called Myrtle, dead now I'm afraid. Lovely name I've always thought - lovely, and you don't hear it much these days."

Myrtle watched him as he put in her address and the details of the cat basket.

"Phone number, Miss Smith?"

"Oh . . . no . . . I don't - "

"Well, you're just right, so you are, they can take over your life."

He put away the laptop and the catalogue. Myrtle's heart jumped - he'd be gone in a minute - should she ask him to have a cup of tea? What could she say? Would you like tea? What about a cup of tea? She stood up and so did he. She tried the words in her head but before she could speak he was holding her hand, shaking it up and down.

"Delighted, Miss Smith, Miss Myrtle Smith."

He pressed her hand harder; his eyes and teeth shone at her.

"Would this day week be convenient for delivery? About twelve?"

Myrtle nodded slowly.

He bowed from the waist and then he left. Myrtle stood at the window, hands clasped together. She had forgotten to take off her old lilac fleece but it didn't matter.

*

The hailstones hurt her face and her fingers were frozen from holding up the hood of the raincoat. If she could just put on her gloves, but her hands were too wet. She had to lean into the wind to walk forward, her breath catching. The sea was black and white and grey and the hailstones fell in silently.

"I wish I was," Myrtle sang, "in Carrick-fer-er-gus."

It was almost dark in the sitting-room when she got home and she turned on the lamps, but it was warm and quiet and she stood still for a minute, savouring the comfort of it. In the kitchen she unpacked the tins - Liver and Bacon, the label said. The cat in the picture was pale yellow with green pointed eyes. Myrtle balanced the tins against the others and put the kettle on.

He'd be here soon. In a minute she'd go upstairs and comb out her hair, put on the black dress and redden her lips.

She dipped her biscuits and curled her toes in the warm socks. Rain hissed in the chimney and the window shook - she'd have to jam it with newspaper, and she would, in a minute. She folded her hands on her stomach, the heat of the tea still in her throat. Her eyes closed, the fire burned, the wind rattled at the window. She could call the cat Bunty - or Bella - or Sammy . . .

The knock at the door frightened her. She sat up looking straight ahead. It was him! She'd have to get up and open the door; she'd have to talk. There was a louder knock; he'd be cold out there, waiting . . . Myrtle stood up and thought briefly about the black dress. She looked at her thick, tennis socks.

"Good morning, Madam, Miss Smith. What a day, what a day."

Silas Bell tried to smile, fighting the wind. There was a parcel at his feet and he picked it up and darted inside. The rain shone on his black hair.

"Cosy in here, Miss Smith, great altogether."

Myrtle stared at the floor.

"And here's your lovely basket. I got the best one there was, the very latest."

He unwrapped the plastic covering and pushed the basket towards Myrtle. It was dark brown; the lining was blue and padded like a dressing-gown.

"Well." Silas Bell stood up.

"Where had you thought of putting it?"

Myrtle breathed loudly; her shoulders were high, her fingers moving.

"Over here in the corner? Or not?"

"Just . . . it'll do . . . just - "

"No, no, we must find a place for the little kitty. It might be better in the kitchen - more heat there at night you know. It holds the heat from the cooker and that. Is it through here?"

He elbowed the kitchen door open. Myrtle put out her hand to stop him but he was already in, looking at the tins of cat food, his eyebrows high on his head.

"What?" He turned to her, swinging the basket.

"Have you got the cat already?"

Myrtle lifted the Trout and Tuna and hit him very hard on the side of the head. He dropped quietly at her feet, his face saying, oh . . . his legs were sprawled out, there was a smudge of blood at his temple and she wondered if he was dead but then he made a sound and moved his hands. She curled his legs neatly and pushed him into the corner.

I'll tell him he slipped, she thought, splashing water on the floor, he slipped on the water and banged his head.

She rolled up a bit of newspaper and stuck it into the rattling window-frame. The black car parked at the kerb shone in the rain. Myrtle looked at it for a minute, shrugged and sat down.

May Toal

There was still thunder in the sky but it was far off now and the rain had stopped. The smell of the earth was strong and Henry breathed it in deeply, liking it. He didn't mind graveyards; it was nice smoking in the dark with no one around. Not for long though - they'd be coming out soon. He might have stayed at home and let her walk. She'd think there was something wrong with him, coming to get her but he had to think ahead. If she had to walk up the shore road in the storm she'd be whinging and complaining; salt spray on her good coat, boo, hoo, hoo, and Henry wanted his dinner early. Was he to be left waiting just because May wanted to trot along to the church with all the other craw-thumpers? Twice a week she went, and money every time.

Henry leaned in close to the grey wall of the church and listened to the singing. He could pick out the odd word - father, soul, heaven. He moved away, back among the graves. He didn't want to be seen when the fools came out and he could hear shuffling now; the singing had come to an end.

A sudden burst of light shone from the main door and people began to come out slowly, talking and stopping and starting. A group of women stood near the porch looking at the sky to see would it rain again and Henry squinted, trying to pick out May's green coat. He felt a spit of rain and wondered if he could get to the car without being seen.

"Godallmighty! Is that you, Henry Toal?"

He heard a laugh behind him.

"I thought you weren't the praying type. I thought you'd go up in a ball of smoke if you were anywhere near the church!"

"Very funny, Barney, very funny. Did you see May about? Is she saying extra prayers or what?"

"Couldn't say, I wasn't in there myself, just taking the short cut. Will you be over for a pint later?"

"Aye, after my dinner."

"See you so. Say one for me while you're at it!"

Jesus! Henry spat his cigarette to the ground when Barney had gone. He'd be the talk of the pub now. That gobshite would be saying all sorts, he'd make a production of it – Henry in among the graves, saying prayers! And where the bloody hell was May anyway? Leaving him like an eejit to be seen by the whole congregation! He stared up and down the street and turned back to the churchyard but it was empty. He took out his phone and rang her but only got the message minder.

"For fuck sake!"

He looked at his watch and stood helpless for a minute. Where could the woman be? Well, he'd soon see what she had to say for herself, and if she said nothing, a few belts would loosen her tongue.

Henry drove home to a dark, lightless house. He turned up the heat and went into the kitchen; the kettle was stone cold. He lit a cigarette and thought about filling it but it wasn't for him to do it. His stomach roared with hunger as he paced the room. What was May at? She must have lied, and she'd got money off him too.

Henry stopped pacing. Maybe . . . maybe she had done this before. How would he know? Money for the collection! By God, he thought, I'll give her a collection. She'll be fucking well collected when I'm finished with her. He began to relish the thought of smacking her good and hard. It was months since he'd hit her; she'd be getting careless; time to sort her out again. She always cried and said she was sorry afterwards. She'd be sorry all right, sore and sorry. Henry closed his fists slowly, watching the muscles jump, but he'd wait till he'd had his dinner.

He put out his cigarette and lit another and then he heard May's step and the swing of the gate. The key was in the door and there she was, pulling off the green coat and patting her hair the way she did. She moved quickly, hardly looking at him, and there was a half-smile on her face. Henry felt his fists curl.

"I suppose you're starving."

May went into the kitchen.

She felt the kettle and threw Henry a look over her shoulder.

"Wouldn't kill you to put it on, you know. You could have had a cup of tea anyway."

She laughed a giddy laugh.

151

"Do you have to stand there staring, Henry?"

Potatoes thick with dirt thudded into the sink. The smell reminded Henry of the graveyard and himself standing there, waiting. And laugh, would she? He moved nearer. Who told her she could laugh like that? She was making it very hard for him to wait. Liar! Well, he had her now all right. His eyes began to water. Don't hit her yet, he told himself. But he couldn't help it - he pushed her shoulder and she staggered. He saw fright jump into her face. Oh, he'd fix her! He stood over her with his arm raised and she hunched away from him.

"What's wrong with you? You leave me alone."

She straightened up and threw half-washed potatoes into a saucepan. Defy him, would she! Henry poked her between the shoulders.

"Tell me more," he said, "about the holy church and the holy priests and all the holy people."

He went round the kitchen after her, turning to meet her, trying to stand in front of her when she put the steaks in the frying pan.

"I like to know where my money's going," he said. "All those collections."

"It was just the same as usual, Henry, that priest that's visiting, Monroe, he's called. Isn't that gas? Do you think he's related to Marilyn? He gave the sermon, better than the usual oul stuff, love your neighbour and all that. There's nothing to tell, Henry, not a thing, unless you want to know what the neighbours were wearing."

Oh, but she had plenty to say for herself, lickity spit, lickity spit, galloping on. Henry slapped her hard; he felt the sting on his palm and she stumbled, reaching out a hand to the sink.

"By God!" Henry caught her by the arm.

"I'm going to find out what you're doing with my money."

He shook her until the permed curls hopped and jumped and tears splashed from her eyes. Behind them the potatoes boiled up and water hissed on the ring. Henry's fingers bit deep.

"I went to the church, May. What do you say to that? I went to say a prayer alongside my wife, but my wife wasn't there. And I phoned my wife but I got no answer. What's up with you now? Speak up, woman! You had plenty to say a minute ago."

He grabbed the wiry curls.

"Ah, don`t. Ah, don`t!" May cried out.

"I went there in the storm," he said into her ear, "to bring you home so you could make my dinner and not be whinging about getting wet."

Henry could feel the heat in his chest burning hotter and hotter. He forced May to her knees, still with his fist in her hair and he never even saw her arm swing up with the saucepan. It cracked against his head and he swayed there with his arms loose.

"Jesus . . . " he said.

When the second blow landed he fell against the table and slid onto a chair. He stared with dopey eyes at May. She'd gone mad, was all he could think.

"Now! Now! Now! Now!" she said. "I'll tell you where I've been if you want to know, not that I could go far on the bit of money you dole out to me."

She laughed suddenly.

"And did you wait there long? I can just see you lurking around and squinting up your oul face. Well, I was in Dinnie's, Henry. Me and your Irene, yes, your sister - we go to talks in the ladies' club, and after that we go to the pub, and after that we get fish and chips and go down to the harbour, and we sit on the wall and eat them. So now you know what the collection's for. It's for me! But you can stuff it up your arse in future because I'm going back to the Civil Service and I won't need your oul money. The girls are gone now and I don't have to be here all the time to cook you steak for your dinner and wash your dirty clothes."

Henry didn't move. He sat there with his fingers twitching and blood coming from his head. He couldn't take in what May was saying.

"You bloody men," she said, "with your big swinging fists. We've been learning things, me and Irene. Did you know that men have to invent things so they can think they're grown up? Rituals Henry, rituals. But not us, Henry. We've got periods!"

May shouted the word at him.

"And having babies, and yous have nothing! Did you know that? All over the world men invent things. They cut their faces and their willies and God knows what else to draw blood."

Henry half-lifted a hand against the spit from her mouth.

"If men had periods," May took a quick breath, "all the oul fellas would be running around the place with bloody sheets - my son is a man, my son is a man - but yous have nothing."

Henry tried to sit up straight, to get his head right. May was smiling fiercely at him. She swung up the pan again and he flinched.

"Now I'm going round to Irene's," she said, "for a cup of tea, or a drink if she has any for I think I need it. You can put up your own dinner, and by Christ, you big gormless shite, you, if you ever touch me again, you're dead."

When the door banged behind her Henry put his hands to the table and pushed himself up. He groped his way to the sink and washed his head with shaky fingers.

"Jesus, God! Jesus, God!"

How could May talk like that to her own husband - about things - she'd no right to talk like that. What sort of a woman was she? He turned off the cooker and lifted the steak onto a plate, and then he drained the potatoes and heeled them out. He tried to eat but when he chewed the cut on his head opened again and he felt a trickle on his face. He lit a cigarette and watched blood drip slowly onto his dinner.

Thelma

"I wonder if I should wash . . . Thelma, do you think I should have a wash?"

Thelma dithered beside the bed, moving from one wee foot to the other, waiting to heave Thomas to his feet. The top of his pyjamas hung open and his belly bulged over the bottoms. There was a line of sweat where the bulge began and another across the back of his neck when he bent to look at his feet.

"Whatever you like, dear. The water's hot."

"Well, I will then. I'll have a nice wash and you can change the bed. I'm a bit sticky. One of the boys spilled beer . . . "

Thomas waved a hand near his pillow and then clutched Thelma's arm. She braced herself and waited while he moved his heavy legs to the floor.

"Up we go," she said. "Upsy daisy."

Slowly, Thomas pushed his feet into his summer gutties and hauled himself up along Thelma's, thin shoulder. She glanced at his jacket hung over the chair, pockets sagging a bit with change, good! Thomas' hand was tight on her wrist and she fixed her eyes on the plump, pink fingers. She would prick him like a sausage . . . prick, prick, prick, all over, and his pink skin would burst open with wee pops and the yellow fat would ooze out, relieved and grateful.

"I'll have a piss first," Thomas said.

"Yes, and have a shower," Thelma said. "You'll feel the better of it."

Thomas nodded and shut the bathroom door. Thelma could hear him coughing, and then he was pissing and spitting and farting and coughing all at once - the whole bloody orchestra, as he said himself. When the toilet flushed she footered about with the socks in his drawer in case he changed his mind and came back but after a minute she heard the shower starting up.

She shook his jacket and pushed her fingers quickly into the pockets. Heavy change - she left a couple of coins so he wouldn't miss the jingle. In his trousers two fivers were stuck together. Thelma took one. She slid the money into one of her green boots with the fur and counted with a quick look. Fifty pounds all told - not bad. She ran her fingers and her eyes over it and then she carefully pulled up the zip. Now, she said to herself, Irene can't say I'm not trying.

A whole weekend away! Up the coast, that lovely, old hotel, and the lovely, soft, sandy beach, not covered in stones like ours! Oh, it'll be great, it'll be magic, magic! She leaned against the chest of drawers with her eyes shut tight and her arms folded, one wee ankle twisted around the other. She'd eat steak and chips and drink Prosecco . . .

She opened her eyes. The bed! She tore the sheet off and pulled at the duvet cover. Crumbs, beer stains, the pillow-case grey from his head. She ran round and round the bed, smoothing and tugging and then she leapt when Thomas roared from the bathroom:

"How long am I supposed to wait here?"

He'd be dripping all over the place! Thelma left the pillow and skipped into the bathroom. Thomas was shivering; he dabbed at himself with a towel.

"What are you like?" Thelma was gay with the money safe and the holiday in her head.

"Come here to me and don't be getting narky."

She grabbed the towel and dried him. He lifted his arms and his fat feet and turned when she told him to.

"Now, don't you feel better?" she said.

"Don't you feel nice and clean?"

"I do," he said, wriggling his shoulders, the skin still a bit damp.

"You'd better get the sambos made. And put the telly on, the boys'll be here soon."

*

"Another twelve? That's it, Thelma? Fifty altogether? It's not nearly enough - it doesn't even approach nearly enough. What have you been doing? It's the middle of July already. When were you thinking of going? Christmas week? Nobody around, nothing going on, wind and rain and cold? It won't do, Thelma. There's others would jump at a weekend in the Glens, plenty of money too, they have, not putting away a few pounds at a time like you."

Thelma shook her head, her wispy, silky hair sliding over her wee face.

"I'm doing my best. You won't let me down now, will you?"

"Ha! Me let you down?"

Irene opened her notebook and tapped the table with her pen. "That's a good one. You've got a nerve, you have. Fifty pounds you've got - do you want to go for one night? One night - take us half a day to get there - "

"But I can get more, Irene. I will, I will get more - you know I will."

She glanced out the window. The boys would arrive soon: plenty of beer - plenty of loose change.

"Well, I don't know," Irene said. "You could try harder, I suppose. He doesn't check every penny you spend, does he? Can't you cut a few corners? Eat a bit less? Give him more bread and less meat."

Thelma shook her head.

"It's all right for you, Irene. You can do what you like - live on bread and jam if you want, sit in the dark and wear a jumper to keep warm if you like. Thomas likes his meat."

"Get a job then. Get yourself up to the supermarket, sit at the till. They *pay* you to do it. Money, Thelma! *Really*, you know, you *really* should come to the classes our Henry's May and I go to. You'd learn a thing or two! If ever a body needed it . . . "

Thelma didn't speak. She stared at the table and shut her ears and squeezed her wee fists on her knee. What would you know, she thought, you with your big hands and your big feet and your hair all screwed up and you don't have a *sausage* in the bedroom shouting orders all the live long day. That's all she ever got - orders.

"Ah for God's sake, there's no talking to you. You know, Thelma, half the time I don't think you're serious about this holiday at all. And I bet you haven't told him yet, have you? You'd better get that over with, quick! Are you afraid of him or what? I'm going to tell you exactly how much you need and then it's up to you. Get a job or get it out of your man in the bed, whatever, I don't care, just get it."

Thelma nodded, and then there was a knock at the door.

"Eh - Irene, the boys are here – I'll have to - "

"Boys! Boys! For God's sake, Thelma. Do you hear yourself? They're men - big lumps of men, expecting you to run around after them, and do you know why they expect you to do that? Because you do it. You do it and you keep doing it and you don't even realise you're doing it. I blame your mother, so I do. She sent you away to that school and all you learned was how to do what you're told!"

Irene swept the notebook and pen into her handbag.

"Up and down them stairs," she said. "Up and down, up and down like a wee skivvy."

She lifted her bag with a swing as the men came in, clattering up the stairs. Alistair said hello, the word slipping out from under his thick moustache.

"Your own brother," Irene said, looking at Alistair's legs in the tight, purple tracksuit. He should be looking out for you. You need to get away - you need to relax. You said you wanted to go, so you did. We'll drink Prosecco you said and eat steak and hire a bicycle maybe and - "

"I know, I know," Thelma said. "Of course I want to go. You know I do. I do"

*

The tray was heavy and Thelma was half-way up the stairs when the door opened and Alistair came out.

"Oh great, the sambos. Here, I'll give you a hand."

He took the tray and turned back up.

"Thanks, Alistair." Thelma flexed her wee fingers. "Are you not staying?"

"Oh I am, of course. Just nipping out to make a few bets. My turn to be messenger. I feel lucky today, so I do, going to make my fortune today. What do you think? And I won't forget my wee sister either," he said.

He kicked open the door and Thelma hovered for a minute, coughing in the smoke. The men reached for the sandwiches, looking at them before biting into them. Thelma set the plates on the bed, her eyes sweeping the floor for money.

"Right then, there you are then, eat up," she said, but no one answered.

Downstairs, she sat in her chair by the window and wondered if she could really work in a shop, a clothes shop maybe. Yes, Madam, that's your colour, definitely . . . would go with anything . . . the teacher at the classes said she could do anything she wanted, all of them could, but the teacher didn't know about Thomas.

From time to time Alistair ran in and out, frowning, serious. And then he came back, laughing. She heard him laughing up the stairs and then there was cheering and stamping. They've won something, Thelma thought. She laughed a bit herself and went up the stairs quickly. There'd be plenty of change tonight; a few beers - they wouldn't notice. Get Thomas out of the room for a bit and then . .

Thomas was sprawled against the headboard, holding a can, smiling.

"Easiest way to make money known to man," he said.

He eased his back and stretched and let his chin fall to his chest. The top of his head shone pink like a rose. Pop, pop, pop; the skin splitting, flesh oozing out slow, blood trickling from his belly, his fingers, his plump thighs . . .

He swirled the beer in the can, tiny drops falling on the clean sheet. Thelma lifted plates and put them on the tray, her eyes all the time on the floor. Easiest way to make money for me! Let yous drop change all over the place after drinking forty cans of beer each. But there was no money on the floor, only bits of sandwich.

And then Thelma had a thought. She stopped at the bottom of the stairs, her mouth open, the tray wobbling. Well . . . why not? It was Alistair's turn - he'd do it for her. She could win hundreds - go away *every* weekend! She could get a nurse in. The tray wobbled again and she scooted into the kitchen with it.

Her fingers shook over the housekeeping purse - how much? She took out a tenner and folded it over and over. Maybe they'd finished betting for the day - they'd already won, hadn't they? The money grew damp in her hand and then Alistair came tearing down the stairs.

"Alistair! Alistair! Will you put a tenner on for me?"

Alistair did a wee jump backwards.

"What's this? What's this?"

"Well, I just want to try it - go on Alistair. Put it on a horse for me, whatever you're backing yourself. Don't be asking me questions."

"But - "

"And don't tell Thomas, don't say anything. Do you hear me, Alistair? Please, will you please?"

"All right, all right."

Alistair shook his head but he took the money. Thelma pushed him towards the door, glancing up the stairs and holding her finger to her lips. She went to her place at the window, her eyes willing him to go faster.

I could be away this time next week! Oh God! What would Thomas say? He'd say go on dear, you

deserve a break, you're a saint the way you put up with me.
I'll be fine, don't you worry, the boys will keep an eye on
me.

No, he wouldn't say that! She tried to imagine his
face when she said it to him - Thomas, I'm off with Irene
for a few days. We're going to drink in dark pubs and eat
chips. Is that all right with you, you lazy, wee shite of a
husband?

She held the curtain to her face and shut her eyes.
She wanted to wrap herself inside it and let them all leave
her alone, Irene and the whole lot of them. How long does
a race take? Her stomach began to burn.

She opened her eyes and dropped the curtain - there
was Alistair at the corner. He was strolling - she thought he
was whistling, hard to tell with that scrubbing brush of a
moustache on his lip. Should he not be walking faster if
she had won something?

He stood at the sitting-room door, his eyebrows
going up and down, nodding and smiling at her. She felt
sick; she thought her heart had stopped. She wanted to cut
off his stupid nodding head and put it on a stick, put it in
the back of a car, nodding and smiling out the window.

"Wait till you see what I`ve got for you!"

Alistair's hands were full of money. He spread it
out like a deck of cards.

"Look at this," he said, laughing.

"We're on a roll - all of us are on a roll today. Hold
your hand out."

Thelma touched the money. "How much?"

"One fifty, Thelma, one hundred and fifty smackeroonies - will I keep some of it back and have another go?"

"No," Thelma said. "No - no - I'll just put it away. Alistair - you're not to tell Thomas, you promised. Not a word!"

Alistair winked and wagged a finger at her and clattered up the stairs.

*

Thelma set down a cup of tea by Thomas's head and then she picked up the empty cans and threw them into the plastic sack. She emptied ashtrays and looked at her own side of the bed. Crisps on the pillow. Thomas was asleep, his head rolling back against the headboard and dropping forward again. Thelma looked at his belly. Drops of blood first and then the skin peeling and popping and the yellow gobs of fat oozing slowly, oh so pleased to be out . . .

Thomas opened his eyes. He lifted the cup of tea and swallowed.

"Would you look at the state of this room!" Thelma said.

Her face was hot and inside she was laughing. She felt warm and safe, all wrapped up and safe. She straightened the sheet around Thomas, brushed off the crisps, her wee feet scurrying from one side of the bed to the other.

"A mess, so it is, this bed."

Thomas pulled a note from under his pillow.

"Here, there's a twenty for yourself. You're a grand wee woman and we had a win today. Don't be always giving out."

"Ah, Thomas, thanks. That's great, I'll put it in my purse in a minute."

Tell him now. Say it. Thomas, Irene and I are . . . She stood there willing and willing the words out of her mouth but nothing happened. She brushed Thomas' strings of hair and settled him against the pillow.

"Finish your tea," she said.

And then she pretended to look for something in the wardrobe and she slid the twenty into the boot, her fingers tapping at the notes.

*

"How did you do since?"

Irene's voice was sharp and Thelma looked at her quickly.

"I got more," she said. "I did, I got . . . I got . . . another . . . twenty."

Irene sighed and shook her head. The notebook fell to the table with a slap.

"What!" Thelma said, a sharpness in her voice. "What! Twenty is a lot in one week. Thomas gave it to me himself."

"Did he now, well, did he! Considering the running around you do, up and down those stairs and feeding every corner boy that comes in, twenty's not much. What have you got now? Seventy? The summer's nearly over."

"Just another week or two, Irene. Wait another - "

"You're never going to have enough, are you? Maybe for next year you will, not for this one. We'll have to call it off."

"What? Off? What do you mean?"

There was a sudden thump on the ceiling and Thelma stood up.

Irene stood up too.

"There you go," she said. "Up you jump. For the big baby in the bed upstairs. I've never been in this house but that floor up there wasn't attacked - it's a wonder there isn't a hole in it."

The women breathed at each other across the table. Irene looked away.

"You know our Henry's May," she said. "She's booked a holiday cottage in Cushendall, for herself just, without Henry. So . . . so, we were just talking about it, and I'm going with her. You could have come too, but . . . "

Thelma didn't answer. She stood there, poised to dash up the stairs the minute Irene was gone. Irene pushed the chair to one side.

"You can't blame me," she said. "We've been talking about this since April and the way I see it, it's your own fault, altogether your own fault."

168

There was a louder, longer banging from upstairs and Irene picked up her things.

"Better see to the child," she said. "I'm off."

Thelma stood still. Her lips were shaking and she swallowed against the tears. She closed her eyes and thought of the money in her wee, green, furry boot in the bottom of the wardrobe and she wanted to run after Irene but her feet wouldn't move.

She could hear Thomas's breathing on the stairs and she turned to look at him. He was shuffling down in his summer gutties, the laces trailing.

"Woman dear," he said. "What's wrong with you? I've been banging on the floor the last ten minutes."

"Ah, sure," said Thelma, squeezing her wee hands together. "Sure, I'm just a bit tired."

Angela

Even with the lights on in the church there was a darkness, especially before the altar where the coffin rested on a trestle. The stained-glass windows were grey with rain; candle flames smoked in the draughts and threw shadows. If Angela closed her eyes she could imagine that the shadows were rows of nuns and whispering girls and that Isabel and herself were back in the school chapel, shivering in the cold half-dark at early mass.

The congregation stood and knelt and there were sighs and coughs and the rattle of beads. Angela didn't know the half of them, cousins, aunts, uncles. They were all vaguely familiar, not as themselves, but as family members; only her own parents were missing, long gone. She was glad now they were gone, that they hadn't lived to bury a child.

Jesus! What a collection, she thought, looking at the careful coats and the clutched hankies. It was just another day out for them and there'd be whiskey and gossip afterwards. She knew they were all staring at her, saying she was so like Isabel - like two little Japanese dolls with their hair so black - everyone said that. They'd be wondering who Mike was, standing there beside her.

Mike was looking at his shoes and Angela knew he was thinking they were the wrong colour for his suit. He would come as her friend, he had said, not as her partner. As if it mattered.

Nobody here knew him, or his pale, whinging wife. She could see him sneaking a look at his watch and her fingers tensed with the need to nip him. God, she could do with a drink, a hot whiskey with lemon and cloves. Gently she smacked her lips together, almost tasting it.

An alter boy swung the thurible and incense rose in puffs as the priest threw holy water across the coffin. Isabel is inside that box, Angela told herself. She is really inside it. And yet she felt that if she opened it there'd be nothing there. She dropped her head into her hands and tried not to think that Isabel was dead because of her ...

*

Angela sat on the side of the bath and stared at the cockroaches. This was the only place in the school where you would see them. In the new wing everything was bare and clean and too bright and Angela didn't like it but here in the old dormitory the walls were panelled with wood, the windows were small, and the floor some dark colour. The bathrooms were huge and cold; no one went near them at night time and when the snores and sighs of sleeping girls grew loud, Angela got up and walked about. She liked the dark, silent corridors and the blue and red lamps glowing in front of the statues.

She switched the light on and off and watched the cockroaches click and slither on the floor and hoped that Isabel wouldn't come looking for her. She was sick of Isabel; there was no escape except when she was in her own classroom. That was her mother's fault, Angela knew. She would have told the nuns that Isabel was shy and to let her stay near her sister for a while.

Angela stood up and tried to see out the high window. It was open at the top and the night wind puffed in. If she closed her eyes and breathed deeply enough she thought she could smell the sea, her own bit of the sea, at the end of her own street. The orchard stretched away from her, the trees planted in tidy rows, almost bare now, and all bent over with the wind. Overhead the clouds moved quickly and Angela stared at one single star until there was a knock at the door and she turned, banging her head on a shelf.

"Are you in there?" Isabel whispered loudly. "Are you in there, Angela?"

"Jesus!" Angela rubbed her head, almost sobbing.

"I'll fix you this time. I'm going to really to fix you."

She jerked open the door.

"What the hell are you doing out of bed? Leave me alone."

"I'll tell," Isabel said. "And I'll write home on Sunday. You were out of bed after lights out and you cursed."

Angela shoved her sister against the wall and turned for the stairs; Isabel's wail followed her.

"You're supposed to look after me. I don't like being on my own and there's noises and dark things - "

"Jesus! There's six other girls in there and you were asleep anyway."

"I wasn't and I don't care. I don't know those girls and you're to mind me and I'll tell - "

Angela's fingers caught her sister's two arms and nipped and twisted, and when Isabel cried out she squeezed her face hard.

"If you open your gob, I'll kill you," she said.

She lay awake and planned to frighten Isabel into obedience. It should be easy. Isabel was afraid of ghosts . . . a white sheet in the black dark and a whispery voice . . . she'd be no trouble after that. Angela turned her head to the next bed. Isabel was asleep - she was sure of it this time. Slowly she drew the top sheet from under the duvet and got out of bed. When she threw the sheet over her head it almost reached the ground and she groped for the rail at the bottom of Isabel's bed.

"Isabel . . . Isabel," she hissed through the white folds.

She shook Isabel's feet.

"Isabel . . . I am the spirit, Wanata . . . Wanata is my name . . . you must obey - "

She didn't get to say any more because Isabel screamed and screamed with her eyes closed and her head thrown back and Angela had only time to shove the sheet down her bed and try to look half-asleep and worried before two nuns came rushing in.

"It was a dream," they told Isabel. "Only a dream . . . "

And they made Angela sit and hold her hand until she fell asleep again.

In the morning Isabel was pale and quiet and wouldn't eat anything. She trailed around after Angela with sorrowful eyes and she sighed and sighed.

"What's wrong with you?" Angela snapped at her.

"Feck off."

"I want the spirit to come back."

Isabel's face was wet and her fingers clutched at Angela's jumper.

"What'll l do, Angela? I have to find her. She must have wanted me to do something and I screamed and ruined it."

Angela gave her a quick nip.

"Well, if she did you'll never know. You ruined it all right. Maybe you've ruined your whole life."

She smiled as Isabel tried to hide the rush of tears.

*

"But you must stay for the party," Isabel said. "I want you to stay altogether. This is your house too - we could live here together, you know that, and I have to tell you about India."

She put her arms around Angela, trying to hug her.

"I want to tell you everything. I feel sure now I can find Wanata. Just think, oh, just think what it would mean to me after all these years!"

Angela looked at the bright face, the shining eyes. Fool, she thought, pulling herself away. Time you knew the truth.

Later she stood in a corner and watched Isabel floating around the house in a yellow dress. She always wore yellow - the colour of joy, she said. Arms reached out to her and her name was called and she was happy. Angela went to her room early, fed-up hearing the surprise in people's voices:

"Well, you're the spit of each other!"

"You're like a pair of Japanese dolls with that black hair."

"You should come to one of our meetings. We'd be delighted . . . "

Angela went up to bed. She smoked leaning out of the window and waited until the guests had gone and Isabel's door had closed, and then she went back downstairs. There was very little of her own self left in this house; Isabel had filled it with candles and flowers and books.

Beyond the French windows there was a huge, bright moon and a light rain was falling. Angela wanted another cigarette and thought of going out but the door behind her opened and there was Isabel in a yellow dressing-gown.

She laughed:

"I might have known - you're still wandering about in the middle of the night, and I didn't get a minute to tell you about India. I have so many people to see I'll be talked out, but there'll be time tomorrow, loads of time, no hurry."

"Rubbish!" Angela said pushing at the bookcase. "Oul nonsense."

"You may think so, Angela. I can't help that. But you can read my books if you like - I told you before, I'll pick out one or two - "

"No! Listen, Isabel! It's the greatest load of bloody - "

Almost, she tried to check herself as she had many times before but this time her mouth opened and the words rushed out.

"There is no spirit world! You can`t get in touch with the other side - do you hear me? There is no other side!"

Isabel yawned, eyes watering.

"I'm going back to bed," she said. "I'm tired - all that noise earlier. I got used to so much peace - such wonderful, blissful - "

Angela stopped her at the door.

"That night at school," she said quickly. "That night you saw the spirit - "

"Wanata," Isabel said, smiling. "Oh yes, that night, the most important - "

"No!"

Angela gripped Isabel's two arms, her fingers almost pinching.

"There was never any Wanata, it was me with a sheet over my head, the name was out of a comic. I knew you were afraid of ghosts - you wouldn't leave me alone and I was sick of you. I put a sheet over my head and - "

"Stop! Poor, dear Angela. You are so unhappy, that's why you drink so much and it makes you want to hurt me. Tell me what's the matter - I might be able to - "

Angela screamed in frustration:

"You're an idiot, Isabel! Messing around with those people, reading those stupid books. I'm telling you it was me! Me! Me!"

Angela breathed hard. She could feel the heat in her face. She waited for her sister to crumble, to fall into a chair, but Isabel began to tidy the books.

"Go to bed, Angela," she said quietly. "Sleep it off."

*

Angela didn't know the men who carried the coffin. She supposed they were cousins but it didn't matter really. Mike walked behind her, distancing himself, his attention on his phone. The wind had dropped but it was still dark and the rain fell straight down. Across from the grave someone coughed. Angela looked up and saw the woman who had phoned to tell her that Isabel was dead.

"Dreadful thing," she had said. "The driver said she was running. Poor man he was beside himself, on his knees on the road, he was, praying. We were waiting for her, you see. There was a new medium, the best, great reputation, and she was so anxious . . .   "

The woman nodded across at Angela, squeezing her lips together as if to say, so sad, so sorry. Angela looked away from her. She wouldn't be a bit sorry. She'd have great fun getting in touch with Isabel, her and her friends. Everyone wanted to shake her hand and say they were sorry for her trouble. Mike hovered, watching, waiting for them all to move off.

"What'll you do later?" he said then. "Will you go back up to Belfast?"

"No, I'll stay in the house, for a while anyway. It's all mine now. You'll help me, won't you, Mike? With the tea and drinks for this lot? Everything's ready. Stay over, stay for a day or two."

"I'll drive you there but I can't stay."

He indicated his phone:

"I`ll have to hit the road - eh - business to do."

Angela caught his arm just above the elbow and nipped and twisted as hard as she could. Mike`s breath hissed through his teeth.

"Bitch! You'll never do that again," he said.

They drove to the house in silence and then Mike said it was a good size of a seaside property and might be worth a bit if she wanted to sell. Angela didn't answer and didn't watch when he left.

The afternoon passed somehow or other. Angela drank whiskey steadily and passed around the sandwiches. Faces appeared and disappeared.

"Remember me?" a voice said in her ear.

"I'm Eleanor - from school - Eleanor Rigby you used to call me, after the Beatles song, you know? We were in the same dorm for a while. And Thelma Woods is here somewhere, her and Isabel were good friends. Strange girl, your sister . . . do you remember the fuss one year over a ghost or something? She was always going on about it - very strange. Oh, here's Jack, would you like to meet - "

"What do you mean? Isabel was not strange!"

Angela snapped at the woman, taking in the black dress, the white face, the deep, red lipstick. She didn't remember her at all. A tall, blonde, bored-looking man loomed up behind her. Angela nodded at him and turned away.

Oh, these people, these people, she thought, refilling her glass. She battled through, holding on till the last, stubborn relations gave in and agreed to leave her on her own. She shut the door and walked through the quiet house.

"Jesus!" she said, looking at the mess of food and drink, but she left it and went upstairs.

In Isabel`s room yellow clothes still lay on the white bed. Angela held a dress to her face and after a while she lay down on the bed and slept. She woke in the middle of the night, cold as a stone, with the echo of Isabel's voice in her head.

"Isabel?" she said, staring into the dark.

She waited and then she got up. She pulled the duvet round her shoulders and stood at the window. A low moon shadowed the garden. She smoked a cigarette, and when it was finished she lit another one.

Pet

The first time I got really angry was two days ago at lunchtime. I was in the kitchen toasting a ham sandwich when I heard the front door open and Jack's step in the hall. He was soaked, he said. The sea was coming over the wall, he said. He ran upstairs and I went out and saw the flowers - a huge bunch of lilies, all pale and greeny-white and tied with ribbons. Freezing cold

they looked. I knew they weren't for me but there was a card and I watched my hand reach out and take it.

"For Louise, love and congratulations, Jack."

I shoved the card back, biting and biting at the inside of my lip, and then Jack tore back down the stairs, hardly seeing me until I spoke.

"Are the flowers for me?"

"What?"

He stopped and gazed at me.

"No, pet, they're for Louise of course."

"Is she dead?" I said.

Jack drew in a breath and the lilies shook a little. I could see the blood gather beneath his eyes.

"In the name of God, woman, what did you say that for? What kind of a thing is that to say? Especially now!"

"I'm sorry, Jack. I'm sorry, but . . . "

I smiled up at him.

"Lilies are for funerals. When Angela's sister died, there - "

"Louise likes them," he said and he turned his face away from me.

"I've asked her to come round for dinner again tonight. You don't mind, do you?"

He was fussing with the ribbons, tidying them and tucking them in.

"No, Jack," I said. "I don't mind. That's all right, that's fine."

And I smiled and smiled but he wouldn't look at me and I knew I shouldn't have said that about Louise being dead.

"William's away for a few days," he said.

"So we'll have to keep an eye on her. And will you try and cook something nice? Something fresh - nice bit of plaice maybe? Make an effort."

And then he was gone, leaving a scent of aftershave behind him. The toasted ham was cold but I didn't want it anyway. I threw it in the bin and made coffee. I didn't want Louise to come for dinner. I couldn't cope with the two of them together, so big and fair and easy - not like me.

Jack used to call me his little brown mouse; people used to say my hair was the colour of a nut, a chestnut, but Jack said I was a little, brown mouse, and that's the way he treated me, like a little pet he'd amuse himself with when he had time. And now! Now Louise was pregnant and I'd have to put up with him being extra nice to her. In the early days he used to pat my stomach and say - any time now - and then later he decided I was barren. I let him think so and swallowed the pills quietly.

Jack doesn't really want children, he just thinks he ought to have them, like the house and the cars and the boat, and me of course, the wife. I didn't want them myself. How could anybody want them? The way they take over people's lives! I've seen enough women hardly able to walk around, swollen and disfigured and sick - and then the suffering! People are sheep, even Jack, following everyone else and pretending to like the whole business. They have to pretend, otherwise they'd all start screaming and kill each other.

I just wasn't going to cook that evening, or make an effort, as Jack said. In the end I grated some cheese and threw a salad together and then I went upstairs for a shower.

I looked at my reflection in the bedroom mirror. I was perfect, not a stray hair, not a crease or a pull in my clothes. And no colour either. All my clothes are pale - Jack approves of them, calls them subtle. I used to always wear red - crimson and scarlet - I don't like being subtle. I stripped and dropped the clothes on the floor and pushed them out of the way.

Rain rattled on the window in a sudden gust and I opened it. The curtain billowed and the air rushed in and I laughed, lifting my arms, bending my legs.

"For God's sake, woman, what are you doing! Cover yourself up! Do you want to be seen? Do you want to catch your death?"

Jack pulled the window shut and the blind down and I scrambled to the wardrobe, noticing the cold all of a sudden, and I couldn't see what to put on. I was shivering.

"Here!"

Jack threw my dressing gown over and I pulled it on as quickly as I could, my arms getting caught in the sleeves.

"Jack," I said. "Jack, what time is Louise coming?"

"Soon," he said with his back to me.

"What should I wear?" I said. "I can't think . . . "

"Whatever . . . "

Jack sighed and sat on the bed.

"Where's that dress I bought you last?"

"This one?"

I took out a watery yellow dress.

"Is it this one, Jack?"

"Yes. I see you made an effort in the kitchen and produced a salad."

His shoes hit the floor and he disappeared into the bathroom.

When Louise arrived I stayed in the kitchen and listened to them talking in the hall. Louise laughed and I bit and bit at my lip. I wanted to stay in the kitchen and eat on my own. What a luxury that would be!

"There you are," Jack said, and he gave me a glass of wine.

I followed him out, smoothing my hair and the watery dress. Louise looked bigger and fairer than ever sitting there in the firelight. Jack had lit candles too. All he needed, I thought, were the lilies and a coffin. Anger was sticking in my throat again. I knew what he was at. Look, he was saying, if you were pregnant I'd fuss over you like this, flowers and candles and smiles. Even though he thought I was barren he still blamed me for it.

"Hello, Eleanor," Louise said. "Do I smell garlic? I don't think I could manage garlic."

She made a face up at Jack and laughed.

"It's only salad," I said. "You needn't have the dressing."

She smiled at me then too. I could see that she was happy and I wondered about William. He was always away off somewhere, on business, or fishing, he said, but you'd have to wonder. Still, she is pregnant.

"Well?" Jack said. "Are we going to eat now? Do you want another drink?"

"No - well if Louise - we can eat now of course - whatever you . . . "

I carried in the bowls and I was careful but the candle flames wavered as I bent over the table and then, somehow, I saw the garlic dressing tip slowly over and spill towards Louise.

"Steady now," Jack said, reaching for it.

Louise wilted a little, waving her hand in front of her nose. I could feel my skin tighten - I became smaller and darker and their shadows were huge in the candlelight.

"Sorry," I said.

I stepped back and caught my heel on the chair and they watched, waiting for me to organise myself and sit down. Jack dished out the salad and cut the bread and we ate. I hardly listened to what they said - I was trying not to drop anything or rattle cups and I wished and wished for Louise to go home.

"What? Sorry?" I said.

"For goodness sake, pet, are you asleep?"

Jack's voice was kind but his eyes were sharp, like ice. I sat up straighter and tried to be bright then but they were so loud and sure. Louise didn't stay long after that. She ate a pear and drank a small brandy and then Jack drove her home. I waited for ages for him to come back. He'd be sitting in her house drinking coffee and telling dirty jokes. He loved telling dirty jokes, only not to me. At last I went upstairs and went to bed and then I heard the car and I thought of his eyes, like ice.

When Jack doesn't want sex he wears his vest under his pyjamas and he walks around noisily, whistling, as if to say - don't mention the vest or I'll be forced to say something disagreeable - and he gives me that dark smile of his. I get the same smile other nights too, and he tells me things other people do in bed, odd things. I used to dare myself to pass a remark on the vest or ask him what odd thing he'd like himself, but I never did.

"Hello," I said, sitting up, trying to see into his face.

"Yes," he said, pulling his clothes off.

"You might have been kinder to Louise, made a bit of a fuss."

"I was kind," I said. "I tried - "

"Yes," he said again. "You tried to spill the dressing in her lap, spoke not a word - "

I screamed then, well, not screamed, but yelped a bit and he stared down at me. I bit and bit at my lip and he said:

"Stop that nibbling and biting. You're . . . "

He closed his eyes and rubbed his face and I knew he was thinking I was like a mouse, only not his little, brown mouse. He put his pyjamas on over his vest and got into bed.

In the morning I found the pale clothes still lying in a heap on the floor and I kicked at them. Outside the sky was grey and dull and Jack was gone. I didn't want to get up and get dressed and I had a headache.

I opened the bathroom cabinet to get something for it and I looked at the pills. Sleeping pills, headache pills, flu pills, other nameless packets, and pills for blood pressure. How Jack loved his blood pressure - a sign of executive stress, of success. I looked at them and my first thought was that I'd swallow the whole lot myself but after a minute or two I changed my mind and I could feel a laugh bubbling up from my stomach. I couldn't wait for Jack to come home.

"Jack," I began the minute he walked in.

"Yes, pet?"

"I thought we should ask Louise to dinner again in case she's lonely - tomorrow night?"

He looked straight at me, surprised.

"Of course, of course. That's very nice of you, pet. Sometimes I think you don't really . . . well that's nice of you."

"I'll ring her right now."

His eyes moved away from me and I could feel the laugh bubble up again so I didn't say any more. When I phoned Louise she didn't answer for a minute - shocked I suppose - I'd never invited her myself before. I could imagine her staring at the phone like she expected me to pop out of it. When she said she'd come I hung up quickly and leaned against the wall and laughed until the tears came and I pressed my face against a coat in case Jack heard me.

*

This afternoon I made a curry and ordered lilies and I got my sister's girl, Lucy, to put my hair up for me. She's only fifteen and I like her fine, if she'd just shut up about her boyfriend. Paulie, she calls him. Paulie this, Paulie that. When she was finished I looked quite severe. I'd wear red lipstick, I decided, go for drama!

When the time came I went to the bathroom and gathered up the boxes and packets of pills. I felt all right but I couldn't breathe properly - I had to keep my mouth open. In the kitchen I emptied the whole lot into a bowl, popping them out of the tin foil - it was like shelling peas. Then I put them into the coffee grinder and switched it on. They broke up very quickly and fell to powder, much quicker than coffee beans.

The lilies arrived and I put them into white bowls, horrible greeny waxy things. I couldn't decide what to wear for death and then of course there was only one dress that would suit, the tight, black one, my party dress, also my funeral dress. It made my hair look darker and my face whiter. I ringed my eyes with black eye pencil, lathered on the red lipstick. Nothing subtle about that.

The curry was just about ready and I was unwrapping garlic bread when Jack came in.

"I've made chicken curry," I said. "Isn't that all right? Louise likes curry, doesn't she? She can leave the garlic bread."

He didn't answer, just frowned, at my darkened eyes, at the lilies, half-smiling.

"What is all this, pet?"

"Say my name," I said.

"What?"

"Say my name. You never say my name. My name is not pet."

The half-smile disappeared. He smacked the newspaper against his leg and went to poke at the curry.

"I made an effort," I said when he wouldn't answer.

"And I ordered lilies - you said Louise likes them."

And I smiled and smiled, still trying, even then.

"Why are you wearing that dress?"

He was walking in and out of the dining-room, taking off his jacket and tie.

"Do you not - " I began.

But he went off upstairs and then the bell rang and I went to let Louise in. She looked me up and down and then she said:

"Hi Eleanor, where's Jack?"

"He'll be down in a minute," I said. "Have a drink?"

"Not yet thanks. I'll wait . . . I'll wait for Jack."

She sat down and I sat down and I stared and stared at her and never spoke until she shivered and moved and I think she'd have gone upstairs only Jack came down then and I could see them looking at each other with their eyebrows up. There they stood, so big and fair and easy and I was so glad about the curry. I gave it one last good stir and ladled it onto their plates. I took my own from the small saucepan and carried everything in and nothing was dropped or spilled.

*

They're both slumped on the couch with their eyes closed. They haven't moved for ages and I wonder what will happen next. Should I ring the doctor? Or get the police? They won't be able to prove anything. It could have been a suicide pact even, brother and sister die together. Yes. I'll just sit here like a little, brown mouse and say nothing. Of course they mightn't be dead at all. I can't really tell and I'm afraid to touch them. But maybe, this time, I'll be satisfied if they're both very, very sick, enough to suffer for a while . . .

Paulie

I don't know if it was reading Dorian Gray that did it but I
suppose it must have had some influence because suddenly
I felt that all things were possible. I was poised right on the
edge - I just had to begin - and I wasn't going to shrink
from anything, bad or good - I would fill my life with
experiences. Of course Oscar Wilde wasn't perfect - he
didn't like Dickens.

"Oscar Wilde didn't like Dickens," I said to the
mirror.

I swallowed slowly, watching the progress of my
Adam's apple. I was still only counting the hairs on my
upper lip but the hair on my head was thick and fair and the
glasses added a serious look. I tried to see my profile and
was twisting my neck around when I heard my brother
come in. He galloped up the stairs, banging off the walls
and shouting – like a volcano he is. He's always home
around five so I knew I'd have to leave soon to meet Lucy.
I left Dorian Gray to one side and tried to cram in some
homework.

The wicker chair creaked under my weight and I
kicked at the socks and shirts. There's no room for
anything in here - the bed and the chair fill the room. When
I stand up I have to fold down the desk. My name - Paul -
is scratched all over the lid. It's written on the walls too,
and the door and the windowsill. I have posters stuck to the

ceiling: Spain, Russia, South America. At night I lie and look up at them and know that I will see them all; they will all see me.

The Geography book fell open at North Africa and I thought again about doing archaeology. All those tombs and statues, and gold and jewels. And I could just see myself there in the sunshine, perched over a gaping hole in the earth, mud-stained, wearing shorts. I could imagine the heat on my back, and I'd be thin and brown, my hair bleached by the sun, my eyes as blue as - were my eyes blue? I took off my glasses and leaned close to the mirror.

"It doesn't matter," I told myself. "Blue eyes are not obligatory."

I examined the shape of my eyebrows and then I pressed my nose against the glass and tried to see the way my pupils grew smaller and bigger again as I moved my head in the light from the window. Then my brother turned on the radio in the room below and the noise rose and disturbed me. I hammered on the floor with a shoe but I knew I wouldn't be heard and it was time to go anyway.

Sometimes I wished my father was still around. I could have asked him things - about girls, women. There's always women in those foreign places, blonde and tanned with crinkles round their eyes and the dust of old bones on their hands. Well, I'd have to learn on my own - with Lucy. She could be part of my beginning, my experience . . . right now, this very night! I bent swiftly to the mirror. My chin looked a bit narrow so I clenched my teeth and I held my shoulders back.

"I will kiss her tonight," I said. "I will. Here, I begin!"

And I felt a lurch in my stomach as I spoke. People always think they feel things in their hearts, but they don't – it's all in the stomach. On Valentine's Day there should be big red stomachs hanging up in shops, and the cards should say - you are my sweet-stomach, my stomach is all yours, and stuff like that.

I ran down the stairs and went out. The breeze was sharp when I turned towards the pier and the air was snappy. The path shone with sparkles and I tried to slide but it wasn't slippy enough. I felt good though - I always feel good in winter - all that blood leaping and rushing around, keeping me warm. My feet seemed to rise above the footpath and I swung my arms and smiled, feeling the strength in my legs as I walked faster and faster.

There was no sign of Lucy when I got to the sea wall but I was early anyway. I like to be early - it gives me an edge, makes me feel in control. And it gave me time to think about kissing Lucy. What would I do first? Well - I'd wait a bit – I wouldn't do it straight away. We could sit on the wall - and then - well, it was only a kiss - people do it all the time. And where was she? Was she going to be late? Tonight?

I heard footsteps and looked up, ready to smile but it wasn't Lucy. It was a couple with a baby in a buggy. The baby was sleeping and your man had his arm across the girl`s shoulder. I walked quietly behind them. They weren't speaking to each other. They might kiss though, I thought and I could watch, see how it was managed. I followed them for a bit and then the Odd Couple went past. I never

194

knew their names but that's what I always called them to myself. He was so short and stringy looking and she was big and stout and wore a man's coat. No danger of them kissing, I thought.

It was colder now - I could feel the wind stinging my ears and I turned my collar up. The couple with the buggy had disappeared. I stared at the sea, so grey and white, waves rising, smacking against the wall. I had nightmares sometimes about tidal waves; it was the idea of the sea drawing itself back rather than the wall of water rushing forward that did it, the noise it made, a sucking, rattling noise . . . I shivered and shook myself.

"Hi, Paulie."

Lucy! I tried to think quickly. Maybe I would do it straight away after all. I gave her a big smile and hooshed myself up on the wall.

"I didn't see you there," Lucy said. "I thought you were late."

"I'm never late!"

I stared at her flushed face with the long hair falling all around it.

"Well, you might be," she said. "I never know what you're going to do next. You're so odd sometimes."

"What do you mean I'm odd sometimes, I'm never odd. I'm the sanest, most logical person I know."

I held out my hand to her.

"Sit up here beside me."

"No, no," she said, doing little dance steps. "It's freezing. Come on and we'll walk, we'll be warmer."

She put her hands under her arms and went off in the same direction as the couple with the buggy.

"Wait," I called after her. "Come here for a minute, it`s not all that cold."

"It is so," she said. "That wall's covered in frost, you can see it from here. Come on, come on before you freeze the ass off yourself. We'll walk to the lighthouse and back and then I'll have to go home."

"You're not let out long," I said, sliding off the wall.

I was thinking how she surprised me sometimes, saying things like that, and then I thought I'd better say something nice to her before I made my move so I told her she looked very pretty. She turned towards me, smiling, lifting a hand to her hair. Now! I bent forward - and then I swallowed and could only think of my Adam's apple travelling up and down.

"What's wrong with you?" Lucy asked. "You've no idea what you look like. I said you were odd and so you are."

She jumped when I put my arm across her shoulders. I gripped tightly, bent down and pressed my lips against hers. They were cold, freezing cold. But then I thought - I've done it! I felt her pushing me away but she was laughing so I let her go and stood back and I didn't care what she said: I tried to keep the triumph out of my eyes.

196

"Well?" I said to her.

"Well, what? I knew you were in a funny mood."

I studied her face. She didn't look pleased, or annoyed either - she looked calm. I couldn't help feeling a bit let down. We walked along slowly, not talking. The tide was in and the sea was very high. I hunched my shoulders against the cold and the next thing I knew she was holding my hand. I let her hold it for a while and then I pretended to look at my watch and she had to let go.

We turned back. There was no one around now. Cars passed at a distance and it started to rain, damp and drizzly. Back at the corner Lucy took my hand again and squeezed it.

"See you, Paulie" she said.

"Paul," I said. "Call me Paul."

She kissed my cheek and giggled and then she was gone.

I stood there for a while trying to work out how I felt. I thought I should be elated - and I was for a minute, just after . . . but . . . I wiped the rain off my glasses and walked on and I bought two bars of chocolate and a bag of crisps in the shop. The kitchen door was open when I went in and I rushed up the stairs before my mother could fuss about wet clothes. I flung myself on the bed and looked up at the posters. Then I laughed and leapt up.

"There you are," I said to myself in the mirror. "You did it."

I ate a bar of chocolate and picked up Dorian Gray, and then I looked in the mirror again. My face should be flushed; my eyes should look different - although - was there a touch of new maturity about my expression? Yes, I thought. Yes, definitely. I examined the hairs on my upper lip and considered my wonderful future. I would gad about the world, open up tombs, the bones would tell me their stories.

And I'd live in the wilds somewhere, with a thin, blonde woman with crinkles round her eyes. There'd be strange smells, exotic faces . . . in the desert maybe, the sand stretching for miles and miles. Oh yes, I could almost taste it, gritty in my teeth. I smiled again at my older, more experienced eyes. Maybe in a thousand years someone would dig up my famous remains. I had begun.

Man and Wife

Jim coughed again, a hard, tight bark from the top of his chest. His head jerked forward when Connie's big hand landed on his back and he gulped for breath, waving her hand away. Connie grinned and hit him again anyway. His chest hurt; his eyes watered and tears sat in the long creases in his cheeks.

The beer tasted sweet going down and he took a long suck, wondering if Connie would let him have another one. He looked at her glass and measured the last of her pint. Connie gave him one of her half-smiles and he knew she knew he wanted another drink. He set down his glass as if he didn't care and glanced with pretended interest around the bar.

The usual trio sat on stools, their heads together, Eugene Curran and the Brothers Grimm, and Jim thought that if Connie wasn't with him he might walk over and say hello, what are you having boys? He tried to imagine that . . . they would talk to him about sport and ask his opinion.

A shout from the corner drew his attention. He thought there was a fight starting but it was only a crowd of young fellows, a whole gang of them, shouting and laughing, and pushing and shoving at a slight, fair-haired one in the middle. He looked like he couldn't stand up for himself and Jim's heart beat sore for him.

"Birthday party," Connie said in his ear.

Jim looked again and saw the huge gold key on the table. The fair-haired boy wasn`t being bullied; his friends were teasing him and Jim could see that he was full of drink. The hair was stuck to his head and his face bloomed in the dark corner.

"That boy's not twenty-one."

"Eighteen."

"You have to be twenty-one to get the key."

"No you don't. That was years ago, it's eighteen now. You know nothing."

"He's not old enough. Look at him."

"Time!" Charlie roared, rattling a spoon against a glass. "Come on now."

Barney Madden started picking up glasses. He'd lift it from under your nose, finished or not. Jim held his on his knee.

The crowd in the corner stood up and pulled the birthday boy to his feet, shouting at him to make a speech and he began to talk, leaning on the back of a chair. He seemed to be nearly crying and he shook everybody's hand over and over.

The trio at the bar pocketed their change and went out, leaving the doors to swing behind them, letting in great gusts of cold air.

"Come on now, Connie," Barney said. "Get that into you. Jim, can you do nothing with that wife of yours? Take her away home to bed."

He laughed when he said that and clattered glasses onto the counter.

One by one the young men got up. With the fair one in the middle carrying the huge gold key they pushed through the swing doors and then they were gone.

"Now, Barney," Connie said, and handed over her glass.

Jim nodded and said goodnight and waited for Connie to button up her new brown duffle-coat. It is a man's coat, he thought again, looking at the long sleeves of it and the breadth across the shoulders. Whatever she says, it is a man's coat. I'll say it to her later, get her going. His own grey tweed was threadbare but he was attached to it. Connie wouldn't let him have a new one anyway. She belted the door open and Jim ducked as it swung towards his face. Barney winked at him and locked the door behind them. They wriggled deeper into their coats, turning their faces from the wind, and then Jim pointed:

"Oh, look!"

The fair-haired boy was crouching at the corner, his arms hugged over his thin chest, and him bare as a baby. He turned when Jim and Connie came out and moved towards them with his knees close together.

"The b-b-b-bastards left me."

He sniffed hugely and wiped his face.

"I thought they were going to throw me in the sea! I'm fuckin' freezin' . . . give us a jacket for God's sake, will you?"

Jim looked at Connie. She was laughing, her eyes going up and down the pale, shivering figure.

"Is it your birthday?" she asked. "Where did they go, your friends? God you're a hoot, isn't he Jim?"

"I'll get my fuckin' death out of this, an' me ma'll be waiting and I've no phone."

The boy's voice went up and up.

"Oh Jesus God I'll kill the poxy bastards. Give us something to put on for fuck sake!"

He began to dance around like a boxer, swinging his arms, and then he remembered to cover himself. Connie turned to Jim and he backed away from her, shaking his head. His chest hurt in the cold air and he coughed. She can't make me, he thought. I'm not going to. For a moment the three of them stood there, until bolts were shot in the door behind them.

"Quick," Connie said. "Charlie's still around, cleaning and that. Go on, knock the door."

And then she turned and knocked it herself.

"What's your name, boy?" she said.

"Frank."

"Frankie Pankie," Connie laughed. "Isn't that right, Jim? Frankie Pankie! God, he's a hoot . . . Charlie!" she roared, banging on the door.

"There's a bare-assed bird out here. Let him in. Come on, we know you're there, we know you're not gone yet."

There was no sound from behind the door and then the lights went out. The wind rose with a cruel nip; the sea rolled black and oily beyond the wall and the first drops of rain were blown over Frank. He ran against the stout door of the pub and shouted for somebody to fucking well open up, and then he ran up and down the street listening for a car, for his friends to come back. Connie watched him and Jim stood well behind her, his coat clutched tight.

"Poxy bastards! Frank screamed into the wind.

"Make your man let me in," he said to Jim and Connie. "Yous know him better than me. He must have heard us knocking - they'll have put him up to it, the fuckers. How am I to get home? Lend us the taxi-fare will yous?"

Jim felt the rain on the back of his neck and turned up his collar. Poor bugger, he thought. He looked at the boy's thin legs, white as milk in the dark night, and his arms like strings wrapped around his chest. Jim was cold himself; he wanted to go home to his quiet bed and lie against the warm bulk of Connie's back.

And then he saw Connie taking off her own coat and his breath puffed out in a snigger. What was she at now? She threw it around Frank's shoulders and he seemed to sink under it, bending his knees, trying to get his feet into it too.

"Come on now." Connie marched him quickly away.

"You come home with us, boy. We'll mind you, won't we, Jim? Sure you're only a little chicken. Are you sure you're eighteen?"

She belted Jim's ear and he staggered.

"Some husband you are," she said.

"Letting your wife give up her coat and you walking there wrapped up like a teddy-bear, much good it'll do you, I'll deal with you later."

Jim knew Frank was looking at him, expecting him to say something, to fight back, but he stared at the ground and coughed his hard, tight cough.

Frank turned after Connie. She walked fast with her face up to the rain and the pleats of her long skirt swung from side to side below the coat. Every time a car passed Frank stopped to look but it was never his friends. Jim wondered what they meant to do. They wouldn't know where he was if they came back. He thought of saying that to Connie but his ear smarted. He fixed his eyes on the bare feet under the long brown duffle-coat. They were wet and splashed with mud and they moved quickly.

Connie put her key in the door and shoved it open. She grabbed Frank by the arm and pulled him inside and he stood in the dim hallway pushing one foot over the other. His face was pale and damp and he didn't look drunk any more.

"Come on, come on," Connie said, and he followed her.

"Sit down, lad, sit down."

Jim hovered while Connie turned up the heating.

"Now, my little chicken." she smiled at Frank. "What are we to do with you? Little Frankie Pankie."

"If you'd just - some clothes - and a taxi - that would be - "

"Tea!" Connie said, pushing Jim towards the kitchen. "Warm him up and then - no - tell you what, Jim, we'll give him a bath. Look at the state of his feet, he's filthy, his legs are all muck. He can have tea later."

"I don't want -" Frank began but Jim was quicker.

"Connie, you can't! What about the drip on the - the leak! The whole wall will come down, or the ceiling, or . . . "

He nodded at the far wall. A long dark streak wound its way down from the ceiling, around the standard-lamp, behind the television and disappeared.

Connie shook her hand at him, her eyes fixed on Frank.

"Ah, stop clucking there like an oul hen. It'll be all right. Come on, pet," she said and reached a hand to the cringing Frank.

"I don't want a bath, Missus. I really - "

"Now, now." Connie tugged at the duffle-coat.

"You'll enjoy it. We'll make it nice and hot. Think of that - how warm and comfortable you'll be. And then we'll find you something of Jim's to wear. Jim won't mind, will you, Jim?"

"I'll be having a shower -"

"Ah, shower me ass." Connie cuffed his ear. "Come on now Frankie Pankie - get up out of that chair like a good boy."

"But, Connie!" Jim gave a little jump on the spot.

"Don't you hit me!" Frank tried to straighten himself up.

"I want to go home. It's late - "

Connie snatched the coat from Frank's grabbing hands and laughed and went into the hall. When she opened the front door they all felt the bite of the wind and for a minute they stood and listened to the lash of rain in the dark, empty street. Frank backed quickly into the chair again and Connie threw him the coat.

"Now," she said. "There'll be no more nonsense. You'll have a nice, warm bath and Jim will get you some clothes and then we'll see. Jim, get up the stairs like I told you."

Jim climbed the narrow staircase and went into the-bathroom. He shivered in the chill air. The white walls were dingy and the floor-tiles curled at the edges. What am I doing, he asked himself. God knows there's no stopping her when she gets a notion. Poor little bugger. I think she's mad. Yes, she's mad. I'll tell her that later, get her going.

He laughed quietly to himself and turned on the tap. He looked around the edge of the bath to see if he could find where the leak was. The taps seemed to be shaky, bit of a gap there maybe. The sound of the running water pleased him. He closed his eyes and thought about a waterfall he had seen once on holidays.

And then Frank was standing in the doorway with Connie prodding him forward. His forehead was puckered, his chin wobbled and his toes were curled on the cold floor. Jim wondered if he was going to cry. When he tried to back away Connie was there, grinning at him.

"Come on now, my little chicken. You can leave off the coat. God you're a hoot, isn't he Jim?"

She leaned down to test the water and it rippled the length of the bath.

"Lovely," she said. "That's just lovely. Come on now, Frankie, in you get."

Frank stared at both of them.

"Aren't you going to leave?"

"Ah, don't be daft."

Connie threw the coat onto the landing and Frank crouched in his thin way until she caught his arm and half-lifted him into the bath.

"You'll be warm in a minute," she beamed at him.

"Won't he, Jim? Sit down. Sit down, I said."

Frank lowered himself into the water and Connie laughed and knelt down, leaning on Jim and hauling him down after her. The face-cloth and soap were stuck to the wooden dish; Connie levered them off and dropped them in. Frank sat and hugged his chest with his goose-pimpled arms and looked smaller than ever. Connie soaped the cloth vigorously and gave it to him.

"I remember," she said, "when I was little and we all had a bath on Saturday night. We had to wait for the water to heat and even then we only got a couple of inches to sit in, and whoever got out first got the hot towel off the boiler . . . come on, boy," she said to Frank. "Scrub-a-dub-a-dub . . . better off than your lot, Jim, you didn't even have a bathroom."

Jim sat back on his heels.

"Well, we had Saturday baths too, only it was the tin bath and last in had to sit in the dirty water, usually me, being the youngest."

Suddenly he whooped and threw water across Frank's back and shoulders.

"Ma used to throw buckets of water over us. The floor was covered with sacks to soak it up and there was always somebody crying."

"Aye, crowd of whingers, your lot."

Connie splashed water as well, her face lit now with two red cheeks. She began to soap Frank's fair hair, spiky now with the water. A sob caught in the boy's throat and he tried to butt her hands away. Connie smacked his protesting hands and legs, the sounds loud on his wet skin. Jim giggled and squeezed out the face-cloth on Frank's soapy head. Connie held him still in the white bath.

"Now, Jim. Give him a good rinse."

Jim stood up and scooped water until his sleeves were sopping and waves splashed out over his trousers. They ignored Frank' protests. Why doesn't he just let her get on with it, Jim thought. He'd get away sooner if he did.

"What's wrong with you?" Connie asked him.

"Anyone would think you'd never been bathed before. Didn't your mother do it when you were little? Or are you a poor little orphan chicken?"

Jim was suddenly tired of it. He said to Connie that Frank was bathed enough and Connie sighed and stuck the soap behind the taps.

"I want out," Frank said, looking at Jim. "I want to go home."

He scrambled to his feet and half-crouched again. His skin was wrinkled. A soapy film settled on the water and Jim leaned over and pulled out the plug. The water gurgled slowly away. Frank began to shiver.

"Can I have some clothes? Please?"

Connie's face brightened.

"Yes," she said. "We'll dress you up nice, won't we, Jim? What have you got that would fit him?"

Frank moved his feet in the last of the water.

"Just give me something to put on - anything - I'll pay for them. I'll come back tomorrow. I want to go home."

Jim brought him into the bedroom and gave him underwear and a shirt and trousers.

"I'll go down and put the kettle on," Connie said.

Jim followed her down. Leave the poor bugger to dress himself, he thought. He stood in the kitchen waiting for the toast to pop up, watching Connie from the side of his eye. She was smiling hugely, rattling cups and plates and Jim was beginning to wonder where Frank would sleep. There was no bed in the spare room and the couch wasn't very big. He looked at his watch; it was 13.00. The toast shot out of the toaster and Jim caught it. The kettle whistled behind him and Connie wet the tea. She was staring at the fairy buns. They were stale but Jim could see that she was going to put them on a plate anyway.

"He said he wasn't hungry." Jim buttered the toast.

"Of course he's hungry. He's young. Young people are always hungry."

She set the buns out and Jim wandered out to the foot of the stairs, and then the knocking started - loud, bold knocks that shook the door. He ran to the kitchen and stared at Connie with his mouth open and Connie stared back, and then they both ran to the hall. Frank was coming down the stairs two at a time. Connie moved quickly in front of him, her pleats swinging, and she stood at the door with her arms folded.

"Answer it!" Frank yelled. "It's my mates! They've come to get me!"

"You don't know who it is," Connie said. "It could be anybody - knocking at the door this time of night - it could be robbers or murd - "

"It's them!" Frank squealed. "I can hear them. Hi lads! I`m here! I`m here!"

It's them all right, Jim thought. I suppose Charlie sent them up, must have heard us talking to him. She'll have to let him out. He looked at the boy wearing his clothes; the jumper was tight on him and the trousers a bit too short and he was wearing Jim's slippers. When the knocks came loud again he pushed Connie aside and darted to the door. He wrenched it open and shot out into the street. The young men standing there laughed and pointed at him. Their feet were wet; they were carrying their shoes and their trousers were rolled up. One of them swung the big golden key and they peered at Jim and Connie standing in the doorway.

Frank let a roar at his friends:

"You're a shower of shites!"

He didn't look back. He got into the car and banged the door and the others followed. The car drew away quickly and disappeared up the street.

Connie told Jim to close the door and not be standing there like an eejit. Jim thought about telling her she was mad. That'll get her going, he said to himself. He remembered the way Frank had looked at him when Connie hit him outside the bar and he went over and over it in his head trying to see himself hitting her back.

He glanced up at the far wall. Ah, he was right - the stain was worse, much worse. He lifted his hand and pointed but Connie wouldn't look. The hectic flush was paling from her cheeks. Jim sat still and waited.

Eugene Curran

The fire is nearly out and I'm getting cold. Drinking this brandy is doing me no good now; I could drink two bottles of it and still be sober. It's Sunday night again - a whole week since I went to bed in peace. I don't like Sundays - dead days I call them.

I remember I nearly fell that night when I was taking off my trousers but I managed to get myself undressed. The curtains were shut tight and I pulled them open - like sleeping in a godamn tomb with them closed like that. I`ve told her and told her. Sometimes I think she does it on purpose.

It was a calm, quiet night with a bit of a moon and not a sinner about in the street. I stood there looking out the window with not a worry in my head and then I turned to the bed. She was well buried in it and I knew I'd had a bit too much to drink, but a man has to have his bits and pieces and I was going to have my rights anyway.

I footered about with the rubber for a minute and when it was on I wheaked up her night-dress and laid into her. She was holding her breath with her face turned away, holding herself tight and still. I laid in good and heavy and when I was finished I rolled off and gave her a good push. She deserved it, I thought, lying there like that as if I was a stranger. I should have clocked her one but that's not the way I work. She spun over onto her side and her knees came up and her head went down. She was like a spider, rolling itself up when you touch it and not a sound out of her - waiting for me to go asleep; my eyes were heavy all right. I pushed her a bit more and she curled up even tighter.

"What ails you?" I growled at her.

The bit of a moon was shining in and she was white as a ghost in the bed. I could see she was shaking.

"Sshhh ...the child," she whispered, pointing to the wall.

Child, my arse. A big lump of a fifteen year old sleeping his bloody head off. She was more worried about the neighbours, don't I know what she's like? All sweet and good morning, missus. She'd die if they heard anything. However I was too tired to go on with it so I lay down again.

I didn't feel too bad the next morning, considering . . . There wasn't much light in the room and the windows were streaming with rain. I thought I'd heard the lifeboat in the middle of the night but maybe I'd only dreamt that.

There she was, moving about quietly, stooped over as usual. She always stoops - she sort of drops at the knees and pokes her head forward like a hen. It's because she's taller than me. I hoped she wasn't sulking. Sometimes she gets in a huff over the drink and there's no breakfast until I raise my voice.

When she left the room I stretched myself and had a good scratch and went to the bathroom. What has she to complain about? Hasn't she the biggest house in the whole county and only young Pat to look after besides myself? She says he's getting stroppy but sure the lad is a teenager; a fine lad too, handsome, and broad for his age. He'll be like myself one of these days, a brave, fine-looking man. Of course I'm getting a bit heavier now about the neck and shoulders but I can carry that. She'll have to learn to cope with him and not be whinging to me.

I was moving stuff around in the cabinet, looking for a new blade, when I came across a packet of hair-dye. I took it out and shook it. Notions, I thought. At her age! I nearly laughed, and then I sniffed the air, hoping for rashers.

Pat was down before me with a plateful in front of him, eyes glued to his phone as usual.

"That's the boy," I said. "Plenty of grub."

He flicked his eyes at me, not a word out of him. My breakfast landed on the table and I rubbed my hands together.

"Yum, yum," I said, just to see the reaction.

She moved away sharpish and didn't speak. She was eating toast at the work top, her shoulders hunched and the spikes of hair sticking up. I took a gander at the head on her; I suppose you could say she was blonde now. Nobody was going to speak only myself by the looks of it. Well, feck the pair of them. It was a good breakfast, best thing after a feed of drink, a good Ulster fry in the morning.

She started cleaning the table around me but I took my time and then went up for my keys and my jacket. I couldn't find my goddamn keys - I could have put them anywhere. I have a habit of hiding things when I'm under the influence.

I groped about under the chest of drawers but all I pulled out was a shoe, one of hers. There was sand in it and I shook it onto the floor. Then I opened all the drawers and shoved my hands in hoping for the familiar rattle, but what I found was a packet of pills, right in at the back. I pulled them out and had a good look and then I realised what they were. The days of the week were on them and they were nearly finished.

I sat back up on the bed with the packet in my hand. There was heat in my chest like a hot iron. If she was on the pill, and it looked like she was, why was I using goddamn, bloody rubbers? The front door banged and young Pat's bicycle scraped along the path. It was time I left for the office but I couldn't get off the bed. I heard her coming up the stairs then and I dropped the packet back into the drawer.

"Are you all right?" she asked, standing at the door. "You`ll be late."

"There's a packet in there," I said, pointing into the drawer.

"A very *suspicious* looking packet!"

"What?" she said, stepping away from me, putting a hand out in front of her.

"What?" she said again.

But she looked at the exact drawer and I kept my eyes on her. I said again there was a packet in the drawer and I told her to get it. She half-turned to go but I stood up from the bed and pointed and she went and got it. We both stared at the packet with the foil sticking out.

"Is it that?" she said.

"Is it that?" I said after her, using a high voice. "Yes, it's that!"

She laughed then, a thin, tittery sort of sound. There was a heavy beat in my throat and sweat prickled under my oxters.

"What do you mean?" she said.

"It's not suspicious at all."

She kept her head down and her fingers gripped the edge of the drawer.

"It's to regulate my cycle," she said. "What's the matter with you?"

"Cycle?" I shouted. "What cycle? Bi-cycle? Motor-cycle?"

I knew well what she meant but I wasn't going to let on.

"The doctor said I was to take them and - "

I held up my hand and she stopped.

"So," I said, real slow. "How - come - I'm - still - using - rubbers?"

"Well, it's just . . . "

She pushed the drawer shut.

"Yes, go on," I said, bending over her. "It's just what?"

"Well, you know, when you've had a drop too much . . . "

She stood up then and looked straight at me.

"Actually, you're a bit rough sometimes and I'd be afraid they wouldn't work. You've only yourself to blame, yourself and the drink, and you'd no call pushing me last night either. And what were you looking in that drawer for anyway? I can't think what you'd be looking in there for. There's nothing in there belonging to you, it's only my things."

She was backing towards the door as she talked. Oh, she could talk when she liked, the twister, raising her voice, trying to make it look like *I* had done something wrong, like I had no right to drink as much as I wanted, no right to look in a drawer in my own house. I glanced at my watch. This would have to wait.

"I have to go," I said. "Where's my keys? Did you see my goddamn keys? Where'd I put them?"

"They're in the kitchen," she said. "On the window-sill."

I went down the stairs two at a time, got them and went out.

All day I thought about how free she was with Pat at school and me at work, and then of course, I'd be in the pub in the evening. A man has to have his bits and pieces.

I thought about that packet of pills, and the hair-dye. And then I remembered the sand in her shoe that morning, and I didn't like it one bit. So I arranged for a week's leave and when I came home that evening I brought the booze with me, drink at home for a night or two, keep an eye on things. I felt like I had a stone in my belly.

Young Pat was eating his dinner, a fork in one hand and his phone in the other. Good job *she* had no mobile. She had looked for one all right, but what for? Aren't there phones all over the house? It's different for the lad.

"All right, son?" I said, sitting down.

He nodded without lifting his eyes. I opened a can of beer and ate my dinner. She was tense - I could tell by the way she moved - she knew I had my eye on her. Pat went out then and I watched the telly and drank my beer. She was waiting for me to start but I had a plan. I didn't bother with my rights that night and I didn't speak at all.

In the morning she asked if I was sick when I didn't get up and I said yes I was and to bring up tea and toast. I listened to her moving around downstairs.

She came up with the breakfast then and said she was going to the shops and she'd get me some flu pills. I waited till the door banged after her and then I leapt out of the bed and got dressed. I was out the door in five minutes and went the short-cut to the shopping centre. I don't know what I expected but she went into the shops and I trailed around after her and then back home again. I appeared behind her when she opened the door.

"Jesus! she said, leaning against the wall with her hand to her neck. "Where did you come from?"

"Just out for a bit of air," I said, and shouldered past her.

She looked at me so hard her eyes nearly crossed and then she said she was going out again.

"Do you want me to get the doctor?"

"I do not," I said. "What for?"

I coughed and rubbed my forehead and my belly.

"I'm not all that sick."

Out I went again after her. She went to the library, then she went into the pub. There were curtains on the bottom half of the windows and I peered over in over the top. Sitting up at the bar she was, drinking coffee as far as I could see, talking to Julia, and that Brigit one, I hate that bitch, airs and graces - here's me head, me ass is following. I had a notion of her once but that wasn't yesterday nor the day before it either.

What were they talking about, their three heads together? That's what I'd like to know. Half an hour I waited there and I was just about ready to go in when she got herself off the stool and came out.

I did the same thing again - came up behind her when she put the key in the lock. Oh, she was rattled then, the keys fell to the ground and there were big tears sitting in her eyes.

"What are you at?" she whinged at me. "What are you up to? Are you trying to frighten me? You don't look sick to me. You'd be in your bed if - "

"Of course I'm sick. Didn't I say I was sick?"

Young Pat came in from school and I went down to the pub for a quick one. I didn't think she'd go out when he was there. I drank plenty that night - I didn't have to rise for work in the morning. Quiet like a cat she was in the bed beside me, hardly breathing, but I left her alone. She'd be getting nervous now, I thought. By God, she would, wondering what the hell I was going to do next.

The rest of the week was the same. I followed her every day but she never went anywhere she shouldn't have. I popped up beside her all over the place and she began to watch for me, her eyes sticking out of her head, all big and roundy. That was a mistake maybe; she was on her guard. I never left her alone in the house and I placed the phones at an angle so I'd know if she touched them, and when anyone rang her I stood in the hall beside her, smiling and shouting, hello.

Drinking in the house began to get to me. It was all right for a day or two but you couldn't keep that up so I leaned on young Pat. I told him to study more, to stay in and get the head down but he's slippery, that lad: it's not that easy to catch a hoult of him.

*

And now it's Sunday again - another godamn dead day, and here I am drinking this brandy. About an hour ago it started. She was up in the bath and Pat was on the couch watching the match, Down and Donegal it was,

"There you are," I said. "Good lad, good lad."

"Uhuh." He looked up at me and away again.

"Match any good?" I asked, smiling at him. "Who's winning?"

"We are."

"I hope you're doing your homework and never mind the football."

"Yes, Da," he said, quick and short.

"It's company for your Ma to have you here when I'm out."

He didn't answer and kept his eyes on the telly but I heard a sigh.

"She's a bit tired looking these days," I said. "Did you notice?"

"No, Da."

I poked at the fire and opened the paper, and then I tried again.

"Has she been going out? Maybe she's been going out a lot and that's why she's tired. Has she left the house when I'm – "

Pat swung his legs off the couch and lifted the remote control and I shot off the chair and grabbed his jersey.

"Are you listening to me?"

I gave him a shake and tried to keep my voice down.

"You answer when I speak. Is your mother sneaking out of the house when I'm in the pub?"

"No!" he said. "No!"

He pulled himself away and ran upstairs to his room. I tried to hold myself in, my teeth clamped so tight my jaw hurt but I had to do something. I knocked flowers out of a vase with a mighty smack; I lifted her rack of CDs and flung them to the floor.

The door opened and there she was. She stared at the mess on the floor, then at me. Her face was damp from the bath and her hair was wet. She looked - sort of - desperate, I suppose.

"What are you playing at?" I said, balling my fists - although I never laid a finger on her, not once, that's not the way I work.

"Oh for God's sake!" she said.

"I'm not the one that's playing. It's you! Following me all over the place, jumping out at me - you've gone mad, so you have, you need a doctor!"

"Twister!" I roared at her. "Twister! Trying to, trying to . . . "

I couldn't find the words so I pushed her hard. She fell against the fireplace and started crying, really bawling, crying out loud, whooping and sobbing. She sank to her knees and crept into the corner beside the fire and bawled and bawled. I didn't feel one bit sorry for her but what was I to do next? There'd be no getting at the truth with her in that state, and I had to get the truth.

I shoved my hands in my pockets and walked up and down the room. Maybe when I was back at work, I thought, she'd think she was safe. I could take a day off and surprise her, catch her in the act.

"I can't stand this," she cried out suddenly. "I want a separation! I want a divorce. You're stone mad, so you are. I can't go out the door - I never know when you're going to appear. I can't live like this! Do you hear me? I want a separation!"

She broke out bawling again and I stared at her wet face, her nose running and her eyes shut. What? A separation? What? Was she going to run off with somebody, her and her box of pills?

"Well, godamnit, you can't have one!" I shouted at her. "As long as I'm breathing there'll be no separation in this house! Where would you go anyway? And who the hell would have you? Eh? Have you asked yourself that? Who would have you? Is there someone waiting for you? Some lover boy on the beach with sand up his backside? Eh? Eh?"

She was rocking herself back and forth and I was trying to think what else to say when she barked out a laugh.

"I wasn't planning on going anywhere," she said. "I want *you* to go."

"Oh, the twister! Out of my own house? There were more tears flowing now and all of a sudden I thought I'd have my rights. After all, I hadn't gone near her for a week. I caught her by the wrist and yanked her up.

"Come on," I said.

She knew right away what I meant.

"No!" She pulled at my hand and tried to fall down again.

"No! What do you mean, no?" I said, and I pulled her up the stairs, step by step.

I bent down and looked into her face.

"Are you keeping it for somebody else?"

Now! I had asked her straight out. She sat down in a heap near the top, shaking her head. Her eyes were closed.

"Right then."

I pulled her onto the landing.

"It's all for me. Isn't it all - "

"No! You can't . . . will you stop?"

She was wailing again.

"Can't what? Can't have my rights?"

"It's the wrong time of the month."

"Hah!" I said.

I dragged her across the landing and into the bedroom and pushed her down on the bed.

"You're lying! I don't believe you. Show it to me."

She shrieked at me, shaking her head. She was pressed against the headboard with her knees pulled up tight, doing the spider trick again. I went for her dressing-gown but she squealed and tried to fight me, hitting and pushing and bawling. I had opened the locker to get the rubbers out before I remembered the packet of pills. I took them out and flung them at her.

"Who is it? Is it someone I know? Dye in your hair and sand in your shoes! Are you thrashing about down on the beach with somebody other than your lawful husband?"

But she wouldn't speak, just kept shaking her head, tears dripping everywhere. And then young Pat burst in, banging the door against the wall and I jumped back from her.

"Ma! Ma!" he shouted, and he looked like he'd been crying too.

His mother waved him away, her arms moving around like she was trying to swim or something.

"Back off, you pup you," I roared at him.

He turned and bolted down the stairs and out the door.

All of a sudden the anger left me. I didn't know whether I wanted to sleep or get drunk. She was crying quietly now, wiping her face and blowing her nose. I was exhausted - I could do no more, so I came down here and started drinking brandy. Pat came back in a while ago and went straight to his room; there isn't a sound from upstairs now. I have to get up in the morning and go back to work. But I will wait. She can`t be clever all the time. I'll find her out eventually, and when I do, I'll kill her.

THE END

About the Author:

For many years Elizabeth Merry wrote primarily for children, publishing along the way a novel and several short stories. A play for children was broadcast on RTE Radio.

"We All Die in the End" is the result of her writing short stories for adults. Elizabeth has also published poetry in various literary magazines and is currently putting a collection together, "The Red Petticoat".

If you have enjoyed this book - or if you haven't - could you kindly leave a review on: Amazon/Goodreads/Twitter/Facebook, whichever suits. Two or three sentences is fine, and honest feedback is always welcome. Thank you.

Printed in Great Britain
by Amazon